I0623513

TOGETHER THIS CHRISTMAS

TOGETHER THIS CHRISTMAS

Beth K. Vogt

Together This Christmas
Copyright © 2025 by Beth K. Vogt

Published in association with Story Architect. www.booksandsuch.com

All rights reserved. No part of this publication may be reproduced, stored in a retrieval system, or transmitted in any form or by any means—electronic, mechanical, photocopy, recording or any other—except for brief quotations in printed reviews without the written prior permission of the publisher.

No AI Training. Any use of this publication to "train" artificial intelligence (AI) technologies to generate text is expressly prohibited.

Unless otherwise noted, Scripture quotations are taken from the (NASB®) New American Standard Bible®, Copyright © 1960, 1971, 1977, 1995, 2020 by The Lockman Foundation. Used by permission. All rights reserved. lockman.org

All characters and events in this book are fictitious. Any resemblance to actual persons, living or dead, or to actual events is purely coincidental.

Book Cover by Courtney Walsh

Print ISBN: 978-1-962845-29-8

Printed in the United States of America

In loving memory of Aunt Jean,
(1929-2025)
Because the words "Together This Christmas"
mean so much more when I consider
you're spending your first Christmas in heaven
with your Father God who you loved so much.

CHAPTER 1

Unlike some people, New York City didn't bypass Thanksgiving and move right to Christmas. Even after living in Manhattan for three years, Mila—like many other New Yorkers—still loved the Macy's Thanksgiving Day Parade, now less than two weeks away. And no, Santa's appearance at the end wasn't her favorite part. Mila would ignore hints of the upcoming *fa la la la la* and enjoy time with Zane.

"That bag isn't too heavy for you?" Mila nudged her boyfriend's shoulder as they maneuvered through the crowd on Fifth Avenue. Ever considerate, Zane adjusted his pace to accommodate her much shorter stride. While her three-inch heels compensated for her five-foot-nothing frame, there were some things she couldn't overcome.

Zane shifted the yellow bag with the red LEGO trademark and took Mila's hand. "I can manage just fine."

"The real question is, how many hours will you need to put that vintage PAC-MAN Arcade together?"

"You want to help me?" Zane's brown eyes registered surprise.

"That's not a serious invitation. You get too much satisfaction out of completing a model all by yourself."

"Maybe I'll slip a LEGO set into your stocking. Something small for you to start on."

"Already thinking about Christmas shopping?"

"Never too early, right?"

Mila sidestepped a trio of teen girls who talked and texted as they walked. "Agreed."

Because it was easier to agree than talk about what she really thought about Christmas.

"What's next?"

Zane glanced at his watch. "We have a little bit of time before our next activity—"

"Activity? Care to explain?"

"I'll let you guess."

"I didn't even finish my BLT bagel from Black Seed at lunch, so probably not a restaurant." She shook the brown paper bag that held the remaining half sandwich. "Leftovers for tomorrow."

"Up for some window-shopping?"

"Zane, you like the LEGO store, where we just spent an hour and a half, and secondhand bookstores. That's about it for your window-shopping adventures."

"This is a nice view." He pulled her to a stop in front of the iconic Tiffany's windows.

Oh.

"See anything you like?"

"Everything?" She could only hope that single word didn't sound as squeaky to Zane as it did to her.

"Understandable." He moved her to a display of diamond rings. "Do you consider yourself a classic kind of woman? Or perhaps something more dramatic?"

A simple, direct question. So why did it seem so reminiscent of when the high school math teacher called her to the front of the class to solve an algebra problem and the answer evaded her?

She raised her hand to touch the glass but then balled her fist into her coat pocket.

Stay calm. This isn't a big deal.

Not true. Moving toward a marriage proposal from Zane would be life-changing.

Wait until she told Ben about this!

"Mila? What do you think?"

Focus on rings now. Text her best friend about it later. "Oh, I've always liked classic things. Movies. Books. Handwritten notes."

"I've appreciated those notes of yours, and I might learn to like black-and-white movies."

"Sorry I'm not a fan of all the different Batman movies you love."

"Not a deal-breaker." Zane shrugged. "You wear both silver and gold jewelry. Any preference?"

"When it comes to a ring?" Had she been too specific? But then, Zane had moved them in front of this display. "White gold or a mix?"

Such a calm discussion, almost businesslike, while people walked by.

Question. Check. Answer. Check.

Her phone chimed in her purse, high and musical.

That text could wait. Nothing was more important at this moment.

Zane eased Mila's hand into his as he pointed out several rings, his skin smooth against her palm. Asked Mila what she liked about them. Noted her replies with a "hmm." Then, a few moments later, he nodded at the window with a satisfied smile. "We'd better get going."

Mila turned her back on the glittering array of jewels. "Are you going to tell me what's next?"

"I hope you're ready to burn off some calories."

"What—? Wait a minute." Mila stopped in the middle of the sidewalk. "Are we going ice skating?"

"Brilliant deduction." Zane tapped his temple. "You mentioned you'd never been ice skating at Rockefeller Center, even after living here for three years."

"I'm going to be worse than a two-year-old out there on the ice."

"Some toddlers take to the ice quickly. I'll hold you up if I need to. That'll be part of the fun." He motioned her forward with a wink. "We've got reservations, so let's go."

Her phone rang. First a text. Now a call.

"I need to answer this." She retrieved her phone from the depths of her purse. "It's Angie. Probably something about her wedding. I'm on speed dial, since I'm her maid of honor."

Zane guided her to the side and shielded her from passersby.

"Angie? Is everything okay?"

"Mila, where are you?"

"Zane and I are out shopping near Rockefeller Center—"

"Oh, I'm sorry to bother you."

"Are you crying?"

"I was." Angie blew out a loud breath. "I'm not now. I'm just frustrated ..."

Mila ducked her head and covered her ear to block out the city noise. "Sorry, it's hard to hear you."

"Wedding stuff. We can talk later tonight."

Mila scanned the street. "I can find someplace quiet."

"No, it's okay."

"If you're sure ..."

"Absolutely. We'll talk later. Have fun with Zane."

Angie's words sounded off-key, as if someone had tried to play a happy song on a piano and struck the wrong note.

Even as she tossed her phone back into her hobo bag, Mila resisted the urge to redial her friend and demand more details. But if it was a real emergency, Angie would tell her.

It had been a day.

What to do first now—text Ben or check in with Angie?

Mila settled onto her secondhand navy-blue loveseat in her studio apartment, her aching feet tucked up underneath her, a mug of one-third coffee, two-thirds cream settled on the side table.

She didn't want to see ice in any form ever again. Not cubed, crushed, frosted, or shaved. And not within the confines of a skating rink. Ice skating was nothing more than an awkward attempt to not fall while Zane asked, "Isn't this fun?" and small children zipped past her at ridiculous speeds. She'd smiled through gritted teeth as they made their way around the perimeter of the rink several times before Zane took mercy on her and suggested they switch their skates for street shoes.

Her phone chimed with an incoming text from Ben.

Hey.

Decision made about who to talk to first.

Aren't you the chatty one tonight.

> Sorry. Long day. Ransacking the fridge for something decent to eat.

Don't let me interrupt you.

> I won't.

Very funny. I need to call Angie soon.

> Charles and Angie are at dinner. They'll be back here later.

One of the advantages of you all living in Chestnut.

In college, all four of them lived in Colorado. On the same campus. Shared so many of the same adventures. Stayed up late studying and dreaming about their futures. They discussed everything from their favorite movies to their favorite books to what they believed about God— accepting that their faith journeys were different. She'd never admitted to some of the questions she wrestled with back then.

How could it be ten years ago? Ben, Angie, and Charles had stayed in Colorado. Mila ended up back home in Kansas with her mom for a few years and then moved across country to New York. Here she sat, alone in her apartment, wearing a worn-out hoodie that Ben had loaned her years ago. He had no idea she still had it and snuggled in its familiar warmth on nights when she missed Colorado.

Mila shook her head. She was an adult now, all of thirty-two years old, not the odd one out. She'd just made a different choice. The rest of her friend group lived in quaint Chestnut, Colorado, and she chose the big city—and found Zane.

> You'll be here soon for Charles and Angie's wedding. What's going on?

> Looks like there's a marriage proposal in my future.

> Zane dropping hints?

> Would you call window-shopping for rings at Tiffany's a hint?

> Guy has nice taste. But then again, he is dating my best friend.

> Thank you for that.

> He still needs final approval.

Mila couldn't hold back a laugh as she typed her answer.

> Which he will get when we come out for the wedding in a few weeks.

> What if this guy doesn't get my vote?

> I like him. Of course you'll like him.

> Hey, I gotta make it hard on him

> Don't scare him off.

> If he's the right one, he won't be scared.

How many times had she heard that from Ben Kendrick? After their failed attempt at dating when they were college seniors, Ben had appointed himself her protector, confidant, and ultimate judge if a guy was right for her.

Ben was the best. She wouldn't risk their friendship by falling in love with him. He was one of the few people who knew why.

> You find something to eat?

> Stealing Charles's leftover pizza.

> You're such a good roommate. Have you found a replacement yet?

> Hey, Charles and Angie just walked in. They want to know if we can video chat.

> Works for me.

> I'll call you back on my computer.

> Okay.

Mila set her phone aside and retrieved her laptop. Her friends' faces appeared on the screen moments later, and Mila leaned forward with a wave. "It's so good to see you all."

A chorus of hellos greeted her.

Angie spoke first. "How was ice skating?"

Mila groaned as she picked up her coffee. "We won't be regulars at Rockefeller Center, that's for sure."

Laughter greeted her admission.

Mila zeroed in on the bride-to-be. "Angie, what's going on? You sounded upset when you called earlier."

Angie blew out a breath. "I mentioned my wedding coordinator's pregnant with her first baby, right?"

"Yes, but I thought you said she wasn't due until after your wedding."

"She's due in January. Sybil's only thirty weeks, but she called today and said she started having contractions."

Mila took a sip of her coffee. "Is she in the hospital?"

"For now, she's on bed rest at home." Angie twisted a tendril of auburn hair that had fallen loose from her messy bun. "She assured me she can still manage things by phone and text, but her OB warned her that, depending on what happens, she may end up at the hospital in Denver."

Charles put an arm around her, and Angie leaned against him. "I told Angie things will be okay—"

"I feel guilty even worrying about my wedding when she's worried about her baby," Angie interrupted. "I want to tell Sybil to not think about anything but getting to her due date, but there are things we need to finish."

"Well, nothing's happened yet." Mila knew her words were small comfort. "She's a professional, so she knows what she can and can't do."

"What if she ends up having the baby early? I'm working at the high school. Charles and Ben are busy with their business. I can't finish up all the wedding details myself, which is exactly why I hired a wedding coordinator!"

"We are not going to *what if* this situation, Angie. We'll take it a day at a time. If something happens, maybe I can come out early and help you ..."

"You'd do that?" Angie leaned forward so her face filled the computer screen.

"I'm your maid of honor, aren't I? I work remotely, and things slow down in December, so I could just bring work with me."

"Oh, that would be great."

"I'm here to help too, don't forget." Ben waved his hand over Angie's head. "Best man and maid of honor. We've got you covered."

"There you go." Mila settled back on the couch and Angie mimicked her action. "In case of emergency, the two of us equal one wedding coordinator."

Friends came through for one another. After all, Angie had helped her pass more than one college math class. Mila would make sure Angie's wedding was a success. It was a good thing her friend couldn't see her online calendar loaded with color-coded work projects. But that was the truth—work at the nonprofit did slow in December. Just not until right before Christmas.

Time for earlier mornings and later nights, just in case those "what ifs" they weren't talking about came true.

CHAPTER 2

Some things were worth the wait, even if Mila had to count down to the Macy's Thanksgiving Day Parade for an entire year.

She wasn't one for over-the-top celebrations. She didn't make a big deal about her birthday. Fourth of July? She watched the fireworks on TV. She didn't understand people who started listening to Christmas music before Thanksgiving—and she tried to hide the fact she didn't listen to holiday music at all.

Life had changed her first day of college when she'd met Ben Kendrick. She'd found a genuine best friend in the fellow freshman who was ready to celebrate anything and everything—and had always insisted she join the fun.

Like today.

You there?

Yes. You do remember there's a two-hour time difference, right? It's not even 6:30 here.

Ben! No sleeping through our Thanksgiving Day tradition.

What kind of tradition is this when you get to sleep later than I do?

The kind of tradition you wake up for.

Mila set down her mug filled with the necessary more cream than coffee on the tiny side table next to her bed and repositioned her laptop, which was tuned to the parade with the sound muted. She switched her phone so she and Ben could video chat. In just a few seconds, Ben's bearded face appeared, hazel eyes lidded, his dark brown hair sticking up in all directions.

"Good morning. You look tired."

With a wide-mouthed yawn, he rearranged his pillow and tucked an arm underneath his head. "I'm still in bed. This is what happens when we watch the Macy's Thanksgiving Day Parade in two different time zones."

"I admit it was easier to watch the parade together when we went to the same college."

"Right. At least we were both tired."

"What else can we do when I'm in New York and you're in Colorado?" She offered him a smile. "Go ahead and grumble, but our tradition is practically sacred."

Ben chuckled, the sound husky and low.

"Laughing at me, Kendrick?"

"Millie, did I laugh at you when you showed up for your first hike in Colorado in worn tennis shoes, ripped jeans, and a T-shirt?"

Ben Kendrick was the only person who ever called her Millie, and she would occasionally lob the name *Benjie* back at him—only to be reminded that she was not his mother.

"Thanks for not mentioning I was also twenty pounds over-weight back then."

"Didn't notice."

Sure, he didn't. He'd bemoaned her shoe choice, loaned her a gray hoodie that was way too large, said the weather could change with little warning, and then promised she'd be prepared for their next hike.

And she was, thanks to a marathon shopping trip to a local outdoors store. She still had those hiking boots.

"Oh, it's almost time for the parade to start." Mila refocused on her laptop. "It's so cold outside today, all those people must be freezing."

"Can you just tell me what you see this year?"

"Where's the fun in that?"

"If you talk softly, I could probably fall back asleep—" Ben sat up in bed and muffled another yawn when he rubbed both hands across his face.

"That is definitely not watching the parade." Mila slid off her bed and carried her laptop to her miniscule kitchen and set it on the countertop.

"Do you really want to miss all the amazing balloons?" Mila stifled her own yawn. "And stop all the yawning. You're making me tired."

"Sorry. Between Charles and me prepping for the holiday season at Hit the Slopes and his upcoming wedding, we're both exhausted. At least he's still asleep." Ben repositioned his phone so she could see his face. "You having breakfast?"

Mila fought another yawn. "I had a protein shake. Now I want to make a quiche."

"A quiche? For Thanksgiving dinner?"

"No, just for me so I avoid ordering takeout. Zane's family tradition is to go to Porter House Bar and Grill for

Thanksgiving. His mom goes all out and throws a huge party for Christmas."

"You're going to cook while we watch the parade?"

"Last I checked, I was the only one watching the parade." Mila glanced at the computer screen. *Yep.* The parade was passing by as they talked. She leaned against her kitchen counter. "I was thinking ..."

"What?"

"Next year you should come to New York City so we can watch the parade together."

"On the TV?"

"No! We'd get up early to stake out a great spot along the parade route and watch the balloons and performers in real time. Together. At the same time." Mila's attention switched between Ben on her phone screen and the parade on her computer screen. "Brilliant, right?"

"Well, that would solve the two-time zones dilemma."

"Great. It's a plan. You can stay with me."

Ben quirked an eyebrow. "And what would Zane say to that?"

"Nothing. He knows you're my best friend."

"Mila, best friend or not, he won't want me to stay with you."

"Fine. You can stay with Zane."

"I don't even know the guy."

"You'll get to know him at the wedding. Problem solved."

"How about you come here next year, we go to Breckenridge, and you run the Race of the Santas with me?"

And that was a nice change of topic.

"That's your tradition with Charles."

"Well, that's not happening this year either. Angie asked him not to do the run because it was too close to the wedding." Ben settled another pillow under his head. "She also dreamed we ran the race and that Charles fell and broke his ankle and ended up waiting for her in the church in his tuxedo while balanced on crutches."

"Poor Angie. Ever since her wedding coordinator was put on bed rest, she's been so stressed out. I've lost count of how many texts she's sent me."

"But Charles said the coordinator's managing things from home, so that's good."

"Commercial break again." Mila retrieved the pre-made pie crust, eggs, cheese, and ham from the fridge. Why had she suggested Ben come to New York next year? Angie might be having nightmares about her December wedding, but ever since the weekend Zane and Mila had window-shopped for engagement rings, Mila had been dreaming about Zane. And marriage. That *was* Zane's intention, right? He was an upstanding man. Ben had to approve.

"What are you doing for Thanksgiving?" Mila pulled milk from the fridge and shook the carton. Should be enough for the quiche.

"Going to my parents'. Charles and Angie are joining us because my mom knows they're not going out of town before their honeymoon."

"Anyone else going to be there besides your family?" Mila set her phone on the counter.

"My sister Quinn invited Ruby—"

"Ruby?" Mila paused and made eye contact with Ben. "Do I know Ruby?"

"Don't think so. She moved to Chestnut about three years ago. Opened an art gallery in town."

Mila pursed her lips. "She sounds nice."

Ben grimaced and shook his head. "Don't try to pair me up with Ruby."

"What? Is she eighty years old?"

"I didn't say that."

"Well then, she's available." Mila put all the items in order on the counter. "Someone you could date. Ask Ruby to be your plus-one for the wedding."

"None of your matchmaking nonsense before nine o'clock a.m. Mountain Time. You've done it for years, and it's never worked. I'd rather you spoil the parade for me."

"Don't give up on me yet, Ben Kendrick. My match-making skills are finely honed. And you are quite the catch."

Mila could never be the right woman for Ben. But she knew him better than anyone else. Who better to find the perfect match for him?

There was nothing better than Thanksgiving with his family, especially the leftovers the day after.

Ben sat at the desk in his small study off the living room and took a bite of the homemade dinner roll crammed full of turkey, his mom's herbed stuffing, and just the right combination of cranberry relish and mayonnaise.

Living in his hometown with family nearby meant that in addition to holiday celebrations, he also had Sunday dinners with his parents and siblings—those who still lived in Chestnut. Everly, a twin who could claim being the oldest Kendrick by mere minutes, was a TV star in California, and Sawyer, the baby of the family, had joined the military right after high school graduation. Other than Ben, that left Cole—Everly's twin—and Quinn to show up at the weekly family dinners.

Sharing a townhouse with Charles was like sharing a dorm room but with more space. They both liked to cook and there was always takeout if work ran late. Of course, in a few short weeks, Charles and Angie would say "I do." Ben still needed a replacement roommate to help cover rent.

He scanned the December work schedule on his computer screen. The beginning of the month, Charles and he would juggle work at their ski and snowboarding rental shop along with the wedding prep. Then Ben would handle everything while Charles and Angie went on their week-long honeymoon to Hawaii. Ben would cover as much as he could the weeks before the wedding. Christmas Eve they were open half a day, but Christmas Day they were closed. Get a plan. Work the plan.

Ben finished his turkey sandwich with a swig of iced coffee and then switched over to his inbox to answer and delete emails. Seconds later, the front door thudded open.

"Ben! You here?" Charles's voice echoed from the front of the house.

Ben pushed away from the desk and strode down the hallway.

Charles and Angie stood in the middle of the living room. Angie clung to Charles's hand, her eyes red-rimmed.

"Hey, guys. Good to see you—"

Angie held out her phone. "We need to call Mila."

Ben took the phone as he asked, "We need to call Mila because …?"

"Sybil's water broke and she's on her way to the hospital in Denver."

"That's not good." At Charles's pointed stare, Ben added, "Sorry. Stupid thing to say. Before we call Mila, is there any possibility you can get another wedding coordinator to fill in?"

"This close to the wedding?" Angie's question ended on a somewhat shrill note.

"Valid point. Mila it is." Ben glanced at the phone, then handed it back to Angie. It wasn't that late in New York. "Let me use my phone."

Mila answered on the second ring. "A phone call, Ben? What's the special occasion? Did you ask Ruby out on a date? Oh, please tell me you did."

"Very funny." At least he waited to put Mila on speaker until she'd answered. "Charles and Angie are here too. Say hi."

"What's going on?" All humor disappeared from Mila's voice.

"Angie's wedding coordinator is on the way to the hospital in Denver."

"Is the baby okay?"

Angie moved closer to Ben. "She's not having contractions, but her water broke a couple hours ago. Sybil needs to be monitored at a high-level medical facility."

When Angie paused after her explanation, Ben spoke up. "You're being called up for wedding coordinator duty, maid of honor."

"Can you still come out early to help me, Mila?"

"Of course, Angie. Don't you worry about anything. You and Charles will still have your beautiful wedding on the twenty-second."

"Oh, thank you."

"Thank Ben too because he's going to help me."

Ben gestured as if straightening a non-existent tie. "That's right. Now the two of you go relax and let me and Mila figure out a few things." Ben waved the couple away as he switched the phone off speaker mode. "Will you pack your superhero cape and come out to save the day?"

"Last I checked, I don't own a superhero cape, but of course I'm coming to Chestnut. It's in the small print under maid of honor responsibilities, right? Now to figure out my flight."

"I'll pick you up." Ben paced the living room.

"Thanks, Ben."

"Hey, Mila?" He lowered his voice. "I didn't know that doing this—whatever this is going to be—was in the small print for best man duties, so you're going to have to be in charge here, okay?"

"First, I need to figure out what's left to do. But between the two of us, we'll get Charles and Angie married, wedding coordinator or no wedding coordinator."

"Right now, it's no wedding coordinator. That's the problem."

Mila's sigh was soft. "Right. Well, I've got work to do. Once I book my flight, I'll text you the information."

"See you soon."

Ben stared at his phone once he signed off. Mila's early arrival to Colorado equaled an early Christmas present. He'd enjoy it while he could. He was almost certain Zane wasn't going to share Mila after those two were married.

CHAPTER 3

This wasn't how Mila had imagined life going four days after Thanksgiving—and the first day of December.

There was no leftover ham quiche in her fridge.

She had no plans with Zane. Not today or for the foreseeable future. And all they'd managed was brunch with his parents and sisters yesterday before she dove into drafting upcoming blog posts for work.

She attached a bright orange TSA-approved lock to her large teal suitcase. Her shimmery gray-blue maid of honor dress, heels, and jewelry were packed in her matching carry-on bag, and her laptop was stowed in her leather messenger bag. Right now, her work and Angie's wedding were equally valuable.

She retrieved her phone and texted Ben.

See you soon.

Just checked your flight. It's on time.

Thanks for picking me up.

What are best friends for?

Just wait in the cell phone lot.
I'll text you when I land.

Stop telling me what to do.

The intercom buzzer to the apartment's security door interrupted their texts.

Gotta go. Someone's at my door.

ZANE?

Don't think so. He had a business lunch scheduled.

Okay. Text when you board.

Will do.

Mila rolled her larger suitcase behind her and then peered through the peephole at a distorted glimpse of Zane's face.

A frisson of surprise trailed up Mila's spine as she fumbled to unlock the door and stepped back to let him in. "What are you doing here?"

"Nice to see you too." Zane leaned in for a quick kiss.

"I'm just surprised to see you! Don't you have a meeting?"

"I moved it back." He took her hand in his, and the coolness of his fingers seeped into her skin. "I wanted to stop by to say I'll miss you."

"That's so sweet." Mila brushed a few snowflakes from his black hair. "I'll see you in just a few weeks for the rehearsal dinner and the wedding—"

"And we'll be back in time for my mother's Christmas Eve party."

Ah. The Halversons' annual event that Zane had made sure she'd put on her calendar back in October. "I'm looking forward to it."

She'd never confess that the thought of going to a party on Christmas Eve, two days after Angie's wedding, was as appealing as a root canal. Without an anesthetic. He didn't know yet how little she appreciated holiday celebrations. Now was not the time to tell him.

Zane pulled her into a close hug, and his spicy after-shave caused her nose to tingle. Maybe she'd finally found Mr. Right.

Not maybe. She *had* found him.

Zane's kiss lingered on her lips. "I can't convince you to stay here?"

"Very funny." Mila pushed him away with a laugh. "You can help me with my luggage. The carry-on is particularly important."

"Presents?"

He sounded like a little boy who loved Christmas. "No, my dress and shoes for the wedding. Those have to make it to Colorado."

"You'll be beautiful."

"All eyes will be on Angie the day of the wedding."

"I'll be watching you. No one else." Zane leaned in for another kiss.

Mila allowed the moment and then stepped out of his embrace. No more distraction. "You're quite the smooth talker today, aren't you?"

"It's the truth."

Mila checked her Uber app. "My ride is almost here."

"Let's get you downstairs for your ride to Kennedy." Zane managed her suitcases, and a comfortable silence settled between them in the elevator, their hands intertwined.

Once outside, snow pelted the sidewalks. Zane opened the door of her Uber, urged Mila inside as the driver loaded her luggage, and then leaned in for a final brief kiss.

He stooped down to see her again. "I'll miss you."

"I'll miss you too."

"Then stay." He seemed ready to slide into the car and use his most persuasive tactics.

"Now you're being ridiculous." Mila offered him a smile. "Love you."

"Love you too. Text when you land."

"Will do."

Zane shut the door with a final click and stepped onto the sidewalk.

Mila settled in the seat as the car eased into traffic. It was nice to be cared for, even if it did seem a bit like an emotional tug-of-war between Zane's expectations and Angie's crisis.

But in the half year they'd been dating, Zane had been so supportive of her. He respected her career goals. Understood the commitment it took to be a successful content creator for a nonprofit. Yes, she worked remotely, but she didn't goof off. She set business hours for herself and refused to wear pajamas all day.

He hadn't met her mom yet, but they'd talked about visiting her early in the new year. Maybe by then she'd be wearing something special on her ring finger.

And Zane's casual approach to God had been a non-issue so far, because Mila hadn't pushed. She'd changed since college. Her questions had become full-blown doubts. Without the encouragement of her friends' faith, she'd faltered. But she and Zane loved each other. They'd figure it out.

"It's getting messy." The Uber driver spoke as he kept his eyes on the traffic ahead.

Sure enough, the storm whirled white outside the windows, and the wipers beat a sharp staccato against the windshield.

"Let's hope it doesn't delay my flight."

"Nah. You're good. It's early in the season for any real snowstorm and these pilots fly in all sorts of weather."

Hours later, the weather proved the Uber driver had been optimistic. And oh so wrong.

A snowstorm overtook the city, and her flight west, along with hundreds of other flights in New York and along the East Coast, was delayed. And delayed. And delayed. Zane's wish to keep her here must have outweighed Angie's need.

But just as she prepared to text Ben an "it's not happening tonight" message, a weary airline representative finally announced boarding for her flight.

Was this what it was like to be granted permission to board the ark with Noah, his family, and all the animals as gray clouds gathered overhead?

Ben! You still awake?

Yep. Watching TV.

My flight's boarding. But you don't have to pick me up

You plan to walk from Denver to Chestnut? You've never been to Angie's new townhouse.

I'll rent a car.

Coming to get you. Try and rest.

I hate sleeping on planes.

Fine. Get some work done.

Thanks. You're the best.

The best man, right?

Right.

AH4UB.

Always Here For You, Ben.

How many times had he typed the code to her through the years? After a tough college exam. A bad blind date. A failed job interview. Or she'd text AH4UM to Ben.

Always Here For You, Mila.

They were always there for each other. The most loyal of best friends. She could always rely on Ben Kendrick.

Why did she sleep on the flight to Colorado? Mila pressed her hand against the searing crick in her neck and blinked against the thin layer of sand that seemed to coat her eyes. There was nothing she could do about her drool-soaked coat collar.

She hauled her suitcase behind her as she exited the underground train, and the "Welcome to Denver" greeting echoed in her mind. The other bleary-eyed travelers stared straight ahead and swayed forward as the train stopped at the terminal and baggage claim area.

Mila stepped onto the crowded escalator, determined not to doze off surrounded by strangers. She stumble-stepped onto solid ground as people veered left and right around her.

First find her luggage.

Then text Ben again.

"Mila!" He stepped to the side of the barrier with his familiar grin.

Mila tried to move faster toward her best friend, all rugged in his dark jeans, gray thermal Henley covered by a red flannel shirt, and brown hiking boots. And then Ben enveloped her in a warm embrace.

His hug was comfortable. Familiar. And yet something was different. Ben Kendrick had changed since the last time they'd hugged three years ago. He was more muscular, his outdoorsy scent somehow more … Well, someone other than his best friend might call it enticing. His warm chuckle seemed to cause the airport sounds to fade away and cued a soundtrack of her favorite rom-com songs. Mila closed her eyes and relaxed against him. This was nice. She could stay here—

What was she doing?

She opened her eyes, stepped back, and slugged his arm. "Hey! I told you to wait in the pickup lot!"

"And I told you absolutely not." Ben grabbed her rolling suitcase and then slung one arm over her shoulders.

"I'm sorry, Ben. You've probably been hanging around here for hours."

"You're worth the wait, Mila."

"Spoken like a true-blue friend."

There. Best friend zone. They were surrounded by the normal airport sounds—computerized voice announcements, the blend of other people's laughter and greetings, and luggage dumped onto the multiple circling conveyer belts.

Her larger bag arrived surprisingly quickly, and Ben led the way to his battered blue Jeep. He pulled a gray backpack from the seat behind her. "Here."

She settled the bag in her lap. "Do you need me to get you something?"

"No, it's for you."

"Me? What?"

"Take a look." He started the engine and backed out of the darkened garage parking slot.

"Water." She tapped the Nalgene bottle. "Right. Need to stay hydrated at this altitude."

"Exactly."

"What's in the lunch bag?" She pulled out a handful of assorted candy and gasped. "Lemonheads ... Zotz ... Sour gummies ... Ben, you're the best."

"We've already established that fact."

"You want one?" Mila popped a Lemonhead into her mouth and dumped the handful of treats back into the bag.

Ben scrunched his face and waved away the offer. "None of that stuff for me, thank you."

Mila rummaged around in the pack again. "Gloves?" She rubbed her fingers across the soft, navy-blue material.

"Did you bring any?"

Mila buried her face in her hands and then peeked through her fingers. "You know me too well."

"I can't remember how many times you lost your gloves during college. Is this still a problem in New York?"

"I hate to admit it ..."

"Zane is aware of this habit?"

Mila paused. That was like asking if Zane knew how she drank her coffee with more cream than java. Or how she deleted the duplicate photos on her phone every month. Or how Christmas was her least favorite holiday.

Zane knew all those things. Didn't he?

"Make a wish!" Ben pointed out toward the left.

"Blucifer!" Even in the just-after-midnight darkness, the dark blue stallion statue with lighted orange eyes stood out, rising thirty feet into the air.

"Did you make a wish?"

"Give me a minute ..." Mila closed her eyes. "And ... done."

"You going to tell me?"

Mila stared at her best friend. "Have I ever?"

"Nope. Not once."

"Not about to start now."

It was a silly tradition she'd started in college. Through the years, her prayers had faded to wishing upon a statue. A few of the wishes she'd made as she drove past the stallion statue had come true. Coincidence, of course. For a good semester at college. For a fun spring break. She came back to Colorado ... made a wish ... and was home again.

Or at least the closest thing to being home. Somehow her mom's place in Kansas was nothing more than where they'd landed after her father left when she was thirteen.

Mila twisted halfway to face Ben. "So, about your date for Charles and Angie's wedding ..."

Ben groaned. "Mila, it's too late—or too early—to be discussing this."

"We've got a couple of hours before we get to Chestnut."

"I'm taking you to Angie's new townhome, remember?"

"Right. Soon to be the newlyweds' home—and it's not like the town is that big. And what else are we going to talk about?"

"Work?"

"Boring. Besides, we text about that all the time."

"The wedding."

"Exactly. You should have a plus-one. Ruby sounds perfect."

"You don't even know the woman."

"She knows Angie and Charles, right? Is she already invited to the wedding?"

"Probably."

"Then ask her to come as your date." Mila took a sip from the water bottle. "Wait. Is she dating anyone else?"

"Am I supposed to know this?"

"In a town like Chestnut, you'd know if she was."

Ben snorted. "I can manage my life just fine, thank you."

"Do you realize you're always like this whenever I try to help you?"

"I don't need your help. You're like the Dolly Madison character in that musical you like so much."

Mila groaned. "Dolly Levi in *Hello, Dolly!* Barbra Streisand plays a matchmaker."

"Exactly."

Just like old times with Ben. Give her twenty-four hours and she'd convince him to take Ruby to the wedding.

Lights from a passing car illuminated Ben's face for a moment as he glanced at her. "Hey, I've got a deal for you."

"A deal?" Mila retrieved another Lemonhead from the paper bag.

"You want me to take Ruby to the wedding?"

"Ye-es."

"I'll do it *if* you'll do the Race of the Santas with me next weekend."

"Oh, Ben, that's ridiculous." Mila unwrapped the yellow candy and tossed it in the air, leaning forward to catch it in her mouth. "Ta-da!"

"Very nice."

"Thank you." Mila offered him a small hand flourish. "I know you can't do the race with Charles after Angie's bad dream, but what about Cole?"

"Not an option. He's on call for our parents' medical practice, so he's a no-go. Come on, Mila, 'tis the season and all that."

"I'm here to help Angie, remember? And I still have work. I'm going to be so busy ..."

"It's a half-mile run."

"In Breckenridge wearing a Santa suit!"

"All the more fun!" Ben tapped the steering wheel. "What about this, then? Be Mrs. Claus to my Santa Claus for Chestnut's Christmas Festival."

"Don't your parents do those honors for the festival?"

"They do, but things have been hectic at the medical practice lately. Mom was trying to convince Quinn and Cole to take their place, but—"

"I know, I know. Cole's on call." Mila savored the blend of sweet and sour as the lemon candy melted on her tongue. "If I do it, you'll ask Ruby to be your date?"

Ben scratched at his beard. "Deal."

"Shake on it."

"Fine." He extended one hand, his skin warm against her fingers.

Yet another crazy bargain she'd made with Ben Kendrick, but it was far easier than climbing a fourteener, and they'd conquered more than one Colorado mountain higher than fourteen thousand feet in years past.

Matchmaking mission accomplished in less than ten minutes.

Their laughter filled the car, as each of them declared victory. She was no fan of Christmas, but she'd pretend to be a jolly old lady to help Ben's love life. Who knew where this might lead?

CHAPTER 4

He was an idiot.

Ben stood in the back office of Hit the Slopes and chugged the cup of coffee before it had time to cool. He prayed his second jolt of caffeine in less than an hour would stop him from downing the cup he'd bought for Charles. Maybe even halt the condemnation that had run on constant replay since he'd left Mila at Angie's townhome last night. He'd deposited her suitcases in the foyer. Shared a brief hug—when he'd caught another faint hint of her familiar vanilla and citrus shampoo in her long blonde hair—as he'd promised, "See you tomorrow. Make that later today."

He'd resisted the urge to bang his head on the steering wheel during the short drive through the empty streets of town. The four-word chant began as he parked his Jeep in his garage, walked through the dark house, upstairs to his bedroom, and brushed his teeth, doing a stare-down with his reflection.

I am an idiot.

For years, Mila labeled all their phone conversations, video chats, and text messages as "best friends and nothing but best friends." But the truth was, he loved Mila Maxwell. He'd fallen in love with her when she was a shy eighteen-year-old. Dated her for three all too brief months during senior year, until she'd broken up with him during one of the most embarrassing moments of his life.

And now she was his best friend—*Sorry, Charles!*—and thriving in the business world. Then why, last night when he'd hugged her at the airport, did it almost seem like Mila was willing for more?

I am an idiot.

Zane wouldn't appreciate it if Ben had welcomed Mila to Colorado with a kiss.

"Greetings, partner." Charles arrived with two cups of coffee from Chestnut's Roasting, the local coffee shop. "You're here early."

Ben waved at the matching cup on Charles's desk. "Thanks. I know I'll need the third round."

Charles set the cup next to Ben's already half-empty one. "That bad, eh?"

"You have no idea."

"Angie told me Mila's flight was delayed—"

"The woman coerced me into inviting Ruby as my plus-one for the wedding."

"The woman?" Charles settled into his rolling chair. "This is how you refer to your best friend?"

"You're my best all-Colorado-all-the-time friend."

Charles held his hands up. "No jealousy here."

"You're a good sport." Ben tucked the extra coffee into the fridge for later. "And I don't need a date."

"You got a problem with Ruby?"

"According to Mila, Ruby sounds perfect for me."

"Why would you talk to Mila about Ruby?"

"I can't remember how the topic came up." Ben shrugged. "It's a done deal. I agreed to ask Ruby if Mila agrees to play Mrs. Claus to my Santa Claus at the town's Christmas Festival."

Charles raised an eyebrow behind his dark-framed glasses. "Your parents aren't doing that this year?"

"Mom was trying to convince Quinn and Cole to take over for her and Dad. It's been nonstop at the practice, and she's just not up to it."

"And now you're going to volunteer you and Mila instead?"

"She declined my invitation to join me for the Santa race in Breck."

Charles powered up the laptop on his desk. "When are you going to ask Ruby?"

"She's already coming to the wedding, right?"

"I think? Sybil was keeping track of the RSVPs."

"I've got time now." Ben headed to the front of the shop.

"You're assuming no one else has already invited her. You're not the only single guy in town, dude."

"What?"

"I saw her talking with Kurt earlier—"

"The ski instructor? Shouldn't he be on the slopes?"

"I'm not in charge of his schedule, but I do know we have a family coming in forty-five minutes to pick up their gear."

"Be back in twenty."

It was a short walk to the Eye of the Beholder art gallery. Ruby knelt in the large front window, arranging items around the faux Christmas tree, her shoulder-length platinum hair adorned with a red bow.

Ben rapped on the glass with his knuckles and waved when she glanced up.

Ruby mouthed his name. Smiled and nodded. Set a small angel sculpture beneath the tree and then scooted backward from sight. A moment later, her shop door opened with a jingle of the overhead bell.

"Come on in." She smiled again, her lips a match for the bow in her hair. "Coffee?"

"No, thanks." Ben noted Ruby had a nice assortment of store-bought sugar cookies set up next to half a dozen bottles of water. "I'll take some water."

"Shopping before work?" She handed him a bottle labeled with her filigree store logo.

"No ... um, I heard Angie and Charles's rehearsal dinner is here, not at a restaurant."

"Yes, that was the wedding coordinator's idea."

"Speaking of the wedding coordinator—"

"Is the rumor true?"

"That she's in the hospital in Denver now? Yep."

"What's Angie going to do?" Ruby settled behind her counter.

"She called in reinforcements. Mila, our longtime friend from college, arrived last night to handle everything. She's also the maid of honor. Between the two of us, we'll get Angie and Charles to the altar."

"Let me know if I can do anything besides hosting the rehearsal dinner."

"There is something—"

"Name it."

"I'd hoped you'd be my date for the wedding."

Ruby tilted her head. "*Your* date? Isn't Mila your date?"

"Mila's boyfriend, Zane, might have a problem with that." Ben chuckled. "So, what do you say? Would you like to attend the wedding with me?"

Ruby hesitated as she shuffled a few papers on the countertop. "Well, I did say I'd help out any way I can."

"I'll be busy with some best man duties, but I'll make sure I'm available for dancing."

"I do love dancing."

"That's a yes, then?"

"Why not?"

"Fantastic." Ben stepped back. He sensed Ruby wasn't all that excited about being his date for the wedding. Not that it mattered. It was one event. More like a companion thing. "Do me another favor and let me know if there's something in your shop on Charles and Angie's wedding registry."

"You don't have to do that, Ben."

"Give me a couple of options. You said you'd help me out, remember?"

"I'll email you some ideas."

"Perfect. I need to get back to work and get some skis ready for a family outing."

"Looks like a great day to be outdoors."

"It does, but I just hand out the gear."

"You're here!"

Angie's greeting coincided with the bedroom door slamming against the wall. Mila feigned sleep, complete with a mock snore, her head buried beneath a pillow.

The charade failed. Seconds later, her friend pulled the cover halfway down. Mila rolled over and gripped the duvet in a sudden tug-of-war with her friend. "Hey, I'm sleeping!"

"Girl, we were roommates. You can't fool me." Angie tugged on the blanket again. "It's ten o'clock. Time to get up."

Mila released the blanket and tossed the pillow at Angie. "You win. I'm awake."

"Good." Angie clapped her hands. "Get moving. I've made my list for the day and checked it twice."

"*Ho ho ho.*" Mila sat up and shoved her snarled hair out of her eyes. "Does your list start with breakfast?"

"A quick one. How do pancakes sound? Your choice of maple syrup or some of Charles's honey that he harvested from his hives this year."

"I forgot Charles took up beekeeping."

"Turns out there are several beekeepers in town." Angie shook her head. "Messing with bees? Not my idea of fun, but I love the fresh honey. And I have lots of cream for your coffee."

"May I shower, please?"

"Of course. I'm not a bridezilla who abandons hygiene for the sake of the to-do list." Angie grabbed the blankets and pulled them all the way off, the cool air causing tingles along Mila's bare legs. "We have a dress appointment in town at eleven-thirty, so we have plenty of time. Marta was recommended by Ben's mom. She's an excellent seamstress."

"I get to see your dress in person!"

"You get to see my dress." Angie's cornflower-blue eyes glowed. "Final fitting, so we're bringing it home with us."

Mila was up and out of bed in seconds to hug her. "I'll be ready. There's no way I'll miss that."

"Thank you for coming." Angie held on tight. "I don't know what I'd do without you."

"You'll have the most beautiful Christmas wedding ever!" She gave Angie one last hug. "Now, I need a shower and to eat some serious calories before we seize the day."

Her phone buzzed on the bedside charger.

"That's either Zane or work." She scanned the screen. "Several texts from both. I'll send a few replies—"

"Mila ..."

"It'll take fifteen minutes, maybe less. I got you, Angie." She typed an "I miss you too" text to Zane even as she reassured her friend. "Heading to the shower now. Can you bring me coffee?"

"Yes."

"I'll be ready, even if I skimp on hair and makeup and eat my pancakes in the car."

"You'll be fine."

Mila acknowledged the need to check her email for changes to one account's graphics and responded to an email about the upcoming newsletter, then checked the weather for Chestnut on her app—cold!—grabbed clothes and her toiletries bag, and set her timer on her watch for a five-minute shower. She was nothing if not efficient.

Her phone rang. Zane again.

She didn't have time to talk, not if she was going to make good on her promised fifteen minutes. She tucked her phone in her faux leather hobo bag, thankful when the ringing stopped. She'd call him first chance she could, maybe while Angie was changing into her wedding gown.

As promised, within minutes they sat across from one another in Angie's breakfast nook off her kitchen.

Mila paused over her first bite of syrup-drizzled pancake. "Wait a minute. It's a school day, isn't it? Why aren't you at the high school?"

"I took the day off because you just got here."

"Ah."

"I also talked to the principal, and she's giving me some flex time because of what's happened with Sybil.

Such is the advantage of being a counselor versus a teacher. And then I have time off once my family gets here on the seventeenth."

"While we eat, tell me what we still need to accomplish before your wedding. All the things. Whether your responsibility or what would have been your coordinator's."

Angie set a binder on the table and flipped it open.

Mila used her fingers for emphasis. "Seventeenth, family arrives. Twenty-first, rehearsal and rehearsal dinner. Twenty-second—Zero Hour."

Angie's eyes widened. "You certainly have the schedule nailed."

"I'm lasered in on the countdown now that I'm playing two roles." Mila pulled the binder across the table. "Any update from Sybil?"

"She texted to say the goal is to stop any contractions and to keep the baby safe inside her as long as there's no sign of infection to give the baby's lungs time to mature. It's all very day to day. I told her not to worry about me and that we're praying for them."

"Sybil takes care of herself and the baby. We'll take care of you—and pray for her too, of course." Mila flipped through the pages. "Ah, here it is, the three weeks before the wedding checklist. Very helpful."

"Actually, we need to look at the one-month checklist."

"We do? Why?"

Angie cringed. "Sybil admitted she let a few things slide. Again, I told her not to worry about it."

"We'll figure things out. The good thing is, your wedding party is small, and your guest list is too."

"Agreed." Angie nodded.

"What does your mom say about all this? Is she worried?"

"She knows about Sybil and she offered to come out early, but Fiona has semester finals. I told her you've come to save the day."

Mila sipped her coffee. "Hardly that."

"Exactly that." Angie pushed her plate aside. "Fiona is so excited about being my junior maid of honor."

"I can imagine—and she doesn't need to concern herself with anything but her finals." Mila paused to take a bite of her pancakes. "Have you checked RSVPs?"

"Not recently. I thought the four of us could do that together."

"Sounds good. What about confirming with musicians? Wait, you're having a DJ at the reception—"

"I was going to ask Charles—"

"The information is right here. I'll do it later today." Mila stood and retrieved the carton of cream from the fridge. "Needs just a touch more. What about the cake?"

"We opted for a dessert table, remember?"

"That's right. I love that idea."

"But ..."

"But what?"

Angie twisted a piece of her wavy auburn hair. "I wish I'd ordered a groom's cake for Charles."

"Have you asked the baker if it's possible?"

"I figured this close to the wedding it was too late."

"You don't know until you ask, and the sooner the better. Also something I can handle. What kind of groom's cake did you want?"

"He's so outdoorsy. Loves hiking and kayaking and snowmobiling. So maybe something along that line."

"The number for the baker is in here too, right?" Mila flipped through pages and added the phone number to her notes app. "I'll call her and see if we can meet with her tomorrow."

"Thanks, Mila. That will be fantastic." Angie paused as her phone rang. "Hold on, this is the photographer."

Angie greeted the person on the other end of the call. Nodded. Paled. "Th-thanks for letting me know. Please take care of yourself."

Angie hung up, tossed her phone on the table, and burst into tears.

"Angie!" Mila had stopped the phone from skittering across the tabletop and onto the floor. "What happened?"

"My photographer ... slipped on some ice ..." Angie gulped back a sob. "... broke her wrist. She can't take my wedding photos ..."

"Oh no. Does she have an assistant she can send?"

How could Mila solve this problem? No photographer this close to the wedding? Professional photographers were booked months in advance.

"What am I going to do?" Angie wiped her face with her napkin.

Mila kept her voice calm. "We've just added something else to the to-do list. These things happen. We adjust."

"*These things*? I'm beginning to think I should have eloped."

"Don't talk like that!" Mila reached across the table and grabbed her friend's hands. "I will call every single wedding photographer in Breck and Denver. We'll figure something out. I can always take your wedding photos. I'm pretty good with my smartphone."

Angie gasped.

"It was a joke, Angie. A very lame joke."

Mila would fly a photographer in from New York if she had to.

Just what was helping Angie going to cost her?

For the past five minutes, silence had loomed over the table like a dark cloud over a cartoon character. Enough. Mila waved her hands over her head. "It feels like it's going to rain in here."

Angie half smiled and then giggled.

Mission accomplished.

Mila stood and scraped the remnants of her pancakes into the trash. "I know we're on a schedule, but let's stop by the guys' shop and tell them about the photographer."

Angie paused by the sink. "I could just call—"

"Or you could see your fiancé for a few moments. Share a hug. You'll feel better."

"You're right." Angie stacked a plate in the dishwasher.

Mila pulled Angie out of the kitchen. "Then ignore the rest of the breakfast stuff and let's go."

Thanks to Angie's "we're on our way" text, Charles and Ben met them outside as they pulled up. Ben wore a long-sleeve Henley shirt with the shop logo, while Charles wore a sweater adorned with a crazed Buddy the Elf and the words "Santa. I Know Him!"

"I see Charles has added to his collection of ugly Christmas sweaters."

"At last count, he now has thirty, and that doesn't include the one I ordered him for Christmas. It features a skiing reindeer with real lights wrapped around its antlers."

"No more details, please."

"Hey, nice to see you." Ben opened the door for Mila. "You caught us in between things. What's going on?"

Mila shouldered her purse. "Nothing more than the fact that the wedding photographer broke her wrist, so finding a replacement is now a high priority."

"*Oof.* That's going to be a challenge."

"Come on, best man, help out a maid of honor." She slid her arm through his as they walked toward Hit the Slopes. Even with the customary three-inch heels on her boots, she didn't reach his shoulders. "Any bright ideas besides calling a bunch of photographers?"

"I'm friends with the local sports photographer at the newspaper."

"Great! Call him."

"I did mention Craig takes photos of football and basketball and hockey, right?"

"He owns a camera. He knows how to operate it. You didn't mention he was injured in any way." Mila ticked the three points off on her fingers. "Please, call him."

"As far as I know, he's a walking, talking Andy Warhol with a camera."

"Not quite the look we want for Charles and Angie's wedding. Maybe he knows someone else?"

"I'll let you know what I find out."

Mila leaned in to give Ben a quick hug. She stepped back, only to have one of her boot heels catch on the step into the store.

Ben caught her hand, pulled her away from disaster and into an awkward embrace.

"You two okay?" Charles stood with Angie by the front door of the shop.

"Yeah ... all good. Just clumsy this morning." Mila extricated herself from the double round of closeness.

"Mila, we need to leave if we're going to make it to my dress fitting on time." Angie moved toward her car.

"All set." Mila tossed the two men a smile over her shoulder as she fast-walked back to the car. "See you tonight when we do a quick review of RSVPs and the reception plans."

She needed to be careful hugging Ben because, for some unknown reason, her best friend suddenly made her clumsy.

CHAPTER 5

Ben waited until the car disappeared before going back inside. The store was empty except for their part-time worker, Lainey. She waved toward the back office, which put her extra-long bold red nails on full display. "Charles said to go on back."

"What? Did he call a meeting or something?"

"If he did, I wasn't invited."

Charles spoke as soon as Ben crossed the threshold into the office. "What's going on with you and Mila?"

"Nothing's going on. We're helping you and Angie with the wedding."

"Thank you again for that." Charles pulled a water bottle and a bottle of Mountain Dew from the office fridge and tossed the water to Ben. "Now tell me why there *isn't* something going on with you and Mila?"

Ben twisted off the cap and gulped down a third of the water bottle. "Did you forget Mila's dating this Zane guy?"

"If Mila were dating me—your second-best friend—you wouldn't do anything. But Zane isn't your friend. And as far as I know, she hasn't mentioned the guy since she got here."

"That's where you're wrong." Ben pointed the water bottle at him. "We talked about him on the drive home from the airport. And before she came out here, she told me they were looking at engagement rings."

"You're okay with that?"

Ben shook his head. "No."

"Didn't think so." Charles took small, methodical steps around the office. "You've got a small window of opportunity. She's dating the guy, but she's not engaged yet and he's not your best friend—"

"You do realize you're repeating yourself."

"When a friend is slow to pick up on the truth, sometimes repetition is needed." Charles stopped pacing. "Why did you two break up in the first place? You were good together. Never made sense to me."

"She wasn't in love with me." There was more to the story, but it was Mila's to tell. Not his. "And now you're telling me I should ignore that fact and—"

Charles held up his hand. "You love her, right?"

"Yeah, I do." The admission settled in the air between them and didn't fizzle into smoke. The years between their last date and now didn't change that.

"Then you have one last chance with Mila. Zane doesn't get here until the day of the rehearsal dinner."

Ben nodded at the clock, a silent reminder that they needed to get to work. "Say I ignore the fact Mila's in love with Zane and I decide to go for it. How do I convince Mila to forget about this guy and fall in love with me?"

"By being her best friend ... and more."

Problem number one? The fact that he *was* Mila's best friend. Charles didn't realize that Mila had decided Ben would be her best friend—*and nothing more*—years ago.

"I'm open to suggestions. Between work and your wedding, I'm juggling a lot."

"We can pray about this and brainstorm ideas before any customers get here, and then we'll talk more over lunch."

"Okay, but—"

"Without that word."

Sounded next to impossible.

Charles snapped his fingers. "What if you and Mila arrange a romantic sleigh ride after the rehearsal dinner for me and Angie."

"At this late date?"

"Talk to Tim Hendricks about it. He started running sleigh rides just outside of town. See what he can do, and then set up one for you and Mila too. Tell her that we're thinking about coordinating something business-wise with Tim through the shop."

"Are we?"

"Not a bad idea. Customers might like the idea of sleigh rides. Worth talking about, right?"

"Agreed. Devious—and yet romantic in a Hallmark movie kind of way. Maybe Thursday night would work." Ben waggled his eyebrows. "She's supposed to help me out during the Christmas Festival and play Mrs. Claus to my Santa."

"Nothing inherently romantic about that—"

"We'll spend time together."

"Maybe you can find some mistletoe and plan an impromptu kiss."

"*Plan* an impromptu kiss?"

"You are out of practice, Kendrick."

"With kissing Mila Maxwell—you know it."

Charles clapped him on the back with a laugh. "Operation Kiss Mila Maxwell has begun."

Ten years ago, Ben hadn't known when he'd kissed Mila goodnight that it was the last time he'd kiss her. He couldn't change their past, but now, maybe he had the opportunity to change their future.

The seamstress had decked out her house for Christmas. All the things Mila usually avoided. A balsam fir tree, centered by the large front window, scented the air and had colorful palm tree garland woven through boughs weighed down with ornaments. Soft holiday music played in the background, and red poinsettias flanked the fireplace.

At under five feet, Marta was even more petite than Mila. She greeted them warmly and then told Mila, "Wait here, please, while Angie tries on her dress."

She ushered Angie down a narrow hallway. Ten minutes later, Marta came back and announced, "She's ready," and led Mila to a large back bedroom lined with floor-to-ceiling mirrors.

Angie faced her on a carpeted dais, her hands clasped in front of her. "Well?"

Mila paused in the doorway. "Angie … look at you! I loved your dress from the photos you texted. But seeing you in it—" Mila took a few steps toward her friend.

Angie's gown was classic. Elegant, with its long lace sleeves and fitted bodice with a sweetheart neckline. The skirt billowed out from the waist accented with a delicate belt that twinkled with faux diamonds and pearls.

"Don't cry." Angie's voice quavered a bit, a combination of laughter and tears.

"I can't help but imagine Charles's face when you walk down the aisle."

Angie faced the mirror, so their gazes connected in the mirror, the mid-length train of her gown spread out behind her. "I hope Charles likes what he sees."

"He loves you"—Mila rose up on tiptoe and wrapped Angie in a gentle hug of lace and tulle—"and I bet he cries when he sees you. You're stunningly beautiful."

Mila stepped back as Marta knelt and arranged the train. She and Zane had never talked specifics about their wedding. That would happen once he proposed. But she wouldn't have a Christmas wedding. Zane wasn't overly religious, but other than the elaborate Christmas Eve party Zane told her about, she could only hope Christmas Day was low-key for the Halversons.

"Mila? What are you thinking about?" Angie's question interrupted her thoughts.

"Oh, sorry. Not important."

"You looked pretty serious—"

"I was thinking about me and Zane. What kind of wedding I'd plan."

"That's fun."

"It is, but first the proposal, right?"

"Are you hoping for a grand proposal?"

"From Zane? No, nothing like that. More like a quiet candlelight dinner. Just the two of us." Mila motioned to Angie. "Enough talk about me. This is your moment."

"You haven't seen the final touch yet." Angie held back a grin.

"Your shoes?" Just the barest tips of Angie's kitten heels were visible beneath the hem of the gown.

"No, something else a little more fun."

"Shoes are always fun."

"Says my friend who never passes up a shoe store."

"Or a shoe sale." Mila shrugged as she smoothed out Angie's gown and adjusted her sleeves. "I admit to a bit of a shoe addiction, but I shop sales."

"We can show her now." Angie nodded at Marta, who opened a white box on a side table and removed a snow-white faux fur cape, perfect for a Colorado wedding, and wrapped it around Angie's shoulders so that it flowed over her gown.

"I love this!" Mila touched the soft fibers with her fingertips. "It's perfect."

"I saw one online and couldn't resist. Marta said she could replicate it."

"Now I want one."

"Oh good! I was hoping you'd say that!"

"What?"

"I had Marta make you a shorter cape."

With a quiet smile, Marta revealed a box hidden beneath the cloth covering the table and removed a shorter cape in a rustle of white tissue paper.

Angie draped it around Mila's shoulders. "This is my gift to you for being my maid of honor."

"Angie, you didn't have to do that." Even as she protested, Mila arranged the mini-cape across her sweater.

"I wanted to. Besides, it'll look so fantastic in the wedding photos, don't you think?"

Mila pressed the softness against her face. "How can I argue with that?"

"You can't. That was the plan." Angie's smile lit up her face. "I also bought one for Fiona."

"You have a nice small wedding party, so that keeps things uncomplicated. Me, Ben. Your sister. Charles's cousin Jared."

"We'll try to keep other things simple too."

"I'm here now, which means you're not supposed to stress. Every wedding has its ups and downs, but Ben and I can handle things now."

Her phone chimed in her purse. Work? Zane? She really couldn't ignore him again. Mila took a quick look.

Ben.

I'm right outside. Can you talk for a minute?

Everything okay?

Need to talk about something. #topsecret

Top secret?

I'll be right there.

"Excuse me for a moment—" She waved her cell phone. "I need to deal with this."

"That's fine. Marta needs to check a few things."

Mila double-stepped down the hallway and out the front door to where Ben leaned against the side of his Jeep in the driveway.

"What's going on?"

"Tracking down my partner in crime, um, my partner in wedding planning." Ben removed his sunglasses. "Nice look. A little fancy for jeans, but you pull it off."

"What?"

He tapped her shoulder. "This for the wedding?"

Mila gripped the cape. "I should have left this inside. Are your hands clean?"

Ben raised his hands with a grin. "Sorry. I won't touch you again."

"Did you find a photographer?"

"Still working on it. Needed to discuss something else with you." Ben put his hands behind his back and stepped closer, his voice lowered to a whisper. "We have an assignment from Charles."

Okay, this was ridiculous. The two of them were outside. By themselves. No one was around to cue up background music.

Just play along.

Mila refocused and matched her tone to his. She leaned just close enough so that she caught a hint of his clean scent without their bodies touching. "Some sort of top-secret assignment that requires whispering?"

"Exactly. Are you up for the mission, Maxwell?"

"You can count on me, Agent Kendrick. What are the details of this mission?"

"Be ready at 2100 hours Thursday night. Dress warm. You do know how to dress warm, Maxwell?"

"Gloves are required?"

Ben nodded. "Exactly."

"Care to share any other specifics?"

"We'll be outdoors. That's all I can say now. Spies are everywhere."

"Outside the seamstress's home?"

"You never know." Ben cleared his throat. "One more thing."

"Yessir."

"You look lovely today, Maxwell."

Mila blinked. Ben's hazel eyes darkened so that the golden flecks seemed to shine brighter. His words warmed her like the cape around her shoulders. "Thank you, sir."

He offered her a brief salute. "See you later tonight?"

"Yes. Yes, of course. RSVPs, right?"

"Right. And my mom said we can try on our Christmas Festival costumes tomorrow night. That work for you?"

"Sure."

Another smile and then Ben climbed into his Jeep and drove off with a wave.

What just happened?

Nothing. Nothing at all.

As far as she knew, Michael Bublé was nowhere near Chestnut, Colorado. No way the singer lurked nearby to croon about being kissed on a cold December night while she'd stood near Ben.

CHAPTER 6

Ben might as well be a man on a real top-secret mission faced with the relentless *tick-tick-tick* of a time bomb. Last night had been an exercise in marital math as he and Mila organized the wedding RSVPs while Angie fed them chili and cornbread and then he and Charles picked up an almost-new sofa from a nearby home and dropped it off at Angie's. Hallmark would probably cut that scene from a movie, but there was still hope for the sleigh ride.

Tonight, he and Mila were meeting at his parents' to try on the costumes for the town's Christmas Festival this weekend. How that fit into Operation Kiss Mila Maxwell, he had no idea.

He'd prepared for their time together like he had for their first date ten years ago. Instead of showing up straight from work, he'd run home and showered. Changed into a newer pair of jeans and a dark green T-shirt, covered with a soft flannel in browns and greens that Mila had sent him last Christmas. He'd grown a beard a few years ago, but it seemed a bit extreme to shave it now. That would likely attract questions and jokes rather than produce the desired effect of Mila seeing him as more than her best friend.

Did Zane what's-his-name have a beard? If he did, the guy probably groomed it with some fancy beard oil. Or he went to a barber lounge on a regular basis and had someone shave and condition it for him.

Ben had to compete with a man he'd never met. Who'd done the one thing he'd never been able to do—convince Mila to fall in love with him. He didn't have the disadvantage of being her best friend like Ben. Did Zane even want to replace Ben as her best friend? Or was the guy happy with not marrying a woman who would be his best friend too?

As he left his house to walk to his parents', Ben paused to text Mila.

Headed to my parents'. See you soon.

Great!

Mom said there's dessert.

Nice.

You working?

How could you tell?

You sound distracted.

Only you know how my texts sound.
Finishing up a work project.

I'll leave you to it.

I won't be late.

All good.

The temperature hovered in the twenties, but the fifteen minutes to his parents' home gave Ben time to unwind. Come Saturday night, white lights would illuminate the area, the town aglow with its annual Christmas charm. The time outdoors settled his thoughts. His heart. And afforded him time to pray.

God, I don't want to mess up what Mila has with Zane if it's what You want for her.

Ben rubbed the back of his neck and restarted his prayer.

To be honest, God, I want to tell You what to do. I want You to change Mila's heart. To make her love me. But that's like the Aladdin *movie, right? No making someone fall in love. Not that You're a genie ... I just want a chance to show her that we could be right for each other. This is more than Operation Kiss Mila Maxwell, although I do want to kiss her again. I love her, God. But I'm afraid of losing our friendship if I admit that to her.*

The gravel in Ben's parents' driveway crunched under his feet, and he stopped. He'd loved Mila for years, even after she'd suddenly stonewalled their romance during spring semester of their senior year.

"Come on and admit you had fun today, Ben." Mila had walked beside him and bumped her shoulder against his.

"Fun?" Ben stopped and stared at her, which meant he had to reposition the huge bunny head he'd worn for the better part of the day. "How is you *volunteering* me *to wear a bunny suit that weighs a ton and hop around all day during the Easter egg hunt fun?"*

"The kids loved you, especially once you stopped hopping away from them."

"Those kids mobbed *me. Who do I talk to about cruelty to animals?"*

"Poor Ben." For all her sympathy, Mila kept her distance from him. No hug. No taking his hand. No kissing him back into a good mood. Wait. He needed to take this stuffy, floppy-eared head off. They had to be far enough away from the crowd of kids that no one would be traumatized if ...

He tucked the ginormous bunny head under his arm. Ahhhh. He could breathe and see again. "Where do you want to go eat? Pizza sound good?"

"I, uh, need to get back and work on a paper."

"We can take the pizza to go."

"Ben." Mila stopped. Squared her shoulders. Faced him. "This won't work."

"What won't work?"

"This." She motioned between them. "Us."

Mila had gone monosyllabic on him.

"Did I do something wrong? I'm sorry if I complained too much about being Peter Cottontail."

The rest of the conversation was as awkward and uncomfortable as wearing a bunny suit for three hours while small children he couldn't see tripped him in their race to find hidden plastic eggs.

The next day he'd shown up at her dorm and told her he wasn't going anywhere until they talked things out. Mila explained the real reason why she wouldn't—couldn't—date him.

And best friend that he was, he'd stopped fighting her. Stopped fighting for them.

Here they were, a decade later. He was still in love with her. She was in love with Zane. Ben could only hope it wasn't too late to convince Mila that they were right for each other. For all his humorous "spies are everywhere" talk earlier, he wanted to do this right.

Mila stood outside the Kendricks' house, one of the oldest and largest homes in Chestnut. She had visited several times for Thanksgiving, along with Charles and Angie. Once she'd visited at the beginning of spring break and joined Ben and some of his siblings for a hike. But this was the first time she'd seen his house decorated for Christmas. Waiting inside? Home. A family. A place where memories were made. Protected.

All white lights trimmed the roofline, the old-fashioned kind, not the newer LED type. Electric white candles glowed in the windows at the front of the house too and seemed to beckon Mila inside.

After a few intense hours to catch up on work and even a brief call with Zane, she'd walked over from Angie's, wrapped in the quiet of the evening. Tiny white flakes—one here, one there—teased a coming snowstorm, and the cold air chilled her skin and chased away her tiredness.

Ben opened the front door and stepped outside, his form backlit with a golden glow. "Mom wants to know if you're going to stand in our driveway all night. She understood why you couldn't make it for dinner, and she saved dessert for you."

Mila stayed where she was. "Your home is like something out of a classic holiday movie."

"Mom and Dad like to keep things traditional." Ben drew close and stood beside her, then faced the house, his shoulder brushing hers. "Sometimes I forget to appreciate it."

"This? Your parents? Your family? Don't ever overlook what you have."

"And you say I'm the romantic one."

"This isn't romance, Ben. This is something steady. Something lasting."

"But it lasted because my parents love each other. My grandparents did too. And so did my great-grandparents."

Ben's words chilled her in a different way than the air, more like a sudden arctic blast that had blown in and destroyed the magic of the moment.

"That's very unusual nowadays." Mila tucked her hands in her coat pockets. "You don't even see that kind of love in movies much anymore."

"I've always hoped you'd find you're really a romantic at heart, Millie."

"And you know why I'm not." Mila swallowed back the urge to call what his parents had unattainable. "I don't want a fairy-tale marriage, Ben."

"Zane's not your knight on a white horse?"

"Did you watch *White Christmas* again?"

"Sorry. I forgot your ban on Christmas movies."

Ben nudged her forward with his shoulder. "It's too cold to stand out here and philosophize. Let's get inside."

More holiday perfection greeted Mila inside the Kendricks' home. The Christmas tree stood in the family room, and of course, it was real, not mass-produced. Ben had told her stories about the many family adventures when they chopped down their Christmas tree each year. Another long-held tradition.

Mila had abandoned Christmas trees years ago, content to order a wreath for her door from a company online. It was real too, the scent of evergreen and the bright red bow hiding the fact that behind her door her apartment was bare of any decorations. Her mom had offered her several boxes of family ornaments years ago, including a wooden nativity set she'd played with as a child, but she had declined. Mementos all tied to when her dad walked out on them? No thank you.

Mrs. Kendrick slipped out from the kitchen and pulled Mila into a hug, as if they saw each other every day rather than it having been years. When Dr. Kendrick waved from his deep leather chair, his wife scolded him to come greet her properly.

"Where are your manners?"

"It's fine, Mrs. K. I know he's tired from a busy day at the practice."

"No one's too busy to be polite, especially when it's you. You're like family."

"Since I'm family, I'll go say hi to him."

Ben's dad rose with a chuckle and gave her a hug.

"Everly and Sawyer are the family members who don't bother to come home that often." Ben's older brother, who had the same dark brown hair as Ben, made this announcement as he strolled down the hallway from the kitchen, a laugh softening his words. Even with his dark-framed glasses, there was no mistaking the family resemblance between the two of them.

"Cole!" His mom aimed an evil eye at him as only a mother could. "I can still send you to your room."

"I don't live here anymore, Mom."

"Exactly."

"You wouldn't kick me out until I have some of your apple pie, would you?"

"Keep sassing like that, and I just might."

The easygoing banter was its own kind of welcome to Mila. The Kendricks were who they were, wherever they were, with everyone. They liked each other, and they liked most everyone else.

"Except for liars," Ben had said once. *"My folks don't tolerate lying."*

She'd never forgotten that. She didn't like liars either, which was one reason she still struggled to forgive her father. He'd lied to her mother. For years after he left, Mila's mother struggled to accept the truth—that all his late nights at work were a clichéd cover-up for the months-long affair. The divorce convinced her. Forgiveness? That took much longer than the affair that destroyed their marriage. Their family.

Somehow Mila's mom chose forgiveness. Mila chose to shut the door on those years of her life. Her father was the one who left—she wasn't going to chase after him.

She was fine. She and Zane wouldn't make the same mistakes her parents had. They loved each other, supported each other, but they gave each other space.

Ben stepped forward. "Mom, we're going to try on the Claus costumes before we have dessert. That okay with you?"

Focus, Mila. Focus.

"Yes, son."

"You'd better hope there's some pie left, little brother."

"Ignore him, Benjie. I made two pies. I kept one hidden."

"Mom!" Cole's eyes widened. "That's not fair."

"And now you sound like a middle schooler. I'll cut you a slice while Ben and Mila try on the costumes." Mrs. Kendrick turned to Mila. "Yours is in the guest bedroom, where you've stayed before."

"Thanks, Mrs. K."

"Thank *you*. It's just been so hectic the last few months. I love playing Mrs. Claus even if my husband acts more like the Abominable Snowman—"

"I'm right here." Dr. Kendrick didn't look up from the magazine in his hands.

"I know you are, dear. As I was saying, it's time for us to take a break. I hope you and Ben have fun, Mila."

"I've never played Mrs. Claus before. I'm not much of an actress."

"We don't expect you to be Everly. Being Mrs. Claus for a few hours isn't about acting. It's about sharing kindness and joy for Christmas with the children in town."

"Well, thank goodness I don't have to compete with your daughter's successful TV career."

Kindness she could do. Excitement for Christmas, her least favorite holiday? That would take an Oscar-winning performance.

"Everyone will want to talk to Santa, right? I'm more of a supporting role. The candy cane carrier."

She'd spend the night in Santa's shadow. Make sure kiddos got plenty of sugar. She'd smile and say "Merry Christmas" until her face hurt.

Even if she didn't believe in the merriness of the season.

Ten minutes later, Mila stared in the mirror at a colossal fashion fail.

Mrs. Claus needed a dress do-over.

The outfit was an overdose of red velvet, white fur trim, and one ridiculously large apron that amplified a feather pillow belly.

> BEN KENDRICK, IT'S A GOOD THING
> WE'RE BEST FRIENDS!

> You can't look any worse than I do, Maxwell.

> Wanna bet? Are you wearing an apron?

Glad I'm not. Come on out.

I may never leave this room.

Just meet me in the hallway.

After a quick peek out the bedroom door revealed no one was in sight, Mila stepped into the hallway. She left the bedroom door open to make a quick retreat into the room if someone came upstairs. If she couldn't handle being outside the bedroom, how was she supposed to parade through Chestnut's town center on Saturday?

Ben appeared a few seconds later, clothed in a matching red velvet outfit, his muscular form hidden beneath several layers of padding.

"Ho, ho, ho." He coughed. "I'm going to need to work on that."

"Yeah, work on your jolly there, Santa Baby."

"You look—" He scanned her up and down. "Matronly."

"Thanks for that." She tucked several pieces of her hair underneath the droopy mobcap. "Need to do something about this."

"Yeah, I don't think Mrs. Claus is known for her long blonde hair."

"Ya think? Your brown beard is a bit off there too."

"I hope I can find a better one before Saturday. The one in there"—he motioned over his shoulder toward the bedroom—"is a bit worn. You can see my scruff through it."

Mila stepped forward and turned his face side to side. "You don't have scruff."

"I don't?"

"No. I like your beard."

"I'm glad to hear that." Ben rested his hand against her fingers, pressing them closer to his jawline.

"Um, yeah …" What were they talking about? "Not all men look good with beards … but you do."

"Thank you. If you like it, I'll keep it." Ben reached down and trailed a finger along a loose strand of hair against the side of her face. "It'll be a shame to hide your hair under that silly cap."

A shiver trailed up her spine. She missed the warmth of his touch against her hand. "I thought about cutting my hair …"

"Really?"

"Z-Zane didn't like the idea …"

"I'd love you no matter what you did with your hair." Ben's voice dropped lower as he spoke. His thumb trailed closer to her mouth, almost as if he might caress her bottom lip.

Mila stilled as Ben took a step closer to her.

Ben was going to kiss her.

He couldn't.

She couldn't.

But … what if they did?

"What do you two think of the outfits?" Mrs. Kendrick's voice preceded her up the stairs. "Do they work?"

Ben stepped back even as Mila pressed against the wall behind her and exhaled a shuddering sigh.

"We're good, Mom."

"Yes. We're good." Mila forced a laugh. "Although Ben said he needs a new beard."

"Oh, I forgot to mention we ordered another beard earlier this week. Should be here today or tomorrow. Quinn reminded me how worn out that one was." Ben's mom closed the space between them. "She said your dad looked like a vagrant Santa Claus."

"New beard. Great." Ben tried to tuck his hands in his pants pockets, only to discover the red velvet trousers didn't have any. He rubbed his hands up and down the sides of his legs.

"I ordered a Mrs. Claus wig too."

"That's great." Mila echoed Ben as she tugged the cap off her head, her hair tumbling past her shoulders. "We were just talking about my hair ... I mean, what to do with my hair."

Had she just lied to Ben's mom? No ... no, not really.

"You two change back into your regular clothes now. Pie's waiting."

"Will do. I love pie. No need to wait for me, Ben. I know the way." She ducked into the bedroom. Shut the door. Held onto the doorknob as if Ben might try to open the door and follow her into the room.

She hadn't kissed Ben.

There was no rom-com music playing in the background. She'd turned the elusive playlist in her mind to OFF.

Dating Ben had been a mistake the first time. Kissing him now would be disastrous because one kiss would be enough to recall the kisses they'd shared all those years ago.

No. Kissing Ben would be more than a betrayal to Zane. It would be a betrayal to all she believed in.

She would not fall back in love with her best friend. She knew better.

Loving your best friend was like believing in Santa Claus.

A foolish waste of time.

Mila hesitated to knock on Angie's bedroom door. It was just after eleven, and she didn't want to wake her, but then, what were friends for if not to wake up and help unravel snarled thoughts? The knock was quick, not too loud, in case Angie was asleep.

"Come on in, Mila."

She half opened the door. "Got a minute?"

"Sure." Angie sat up and leaned against the headboard. "Get over here."

With a groan, Mila collapsed across Angie's thick down comforter.

Angie patted her shoulder. "Everything okay?"

"Yes ... no. I guess so."

"That's one muddled answer."

Mila stared at the wall. "Zane and I played phone tag all day. I just listened to his last few messages."

"Oh?"

"He loves me. Misses me." Mila rolled over on her back. "He's disappointed I won't be at his office Christmas party next week."

"If you need to go back ..."

"No! I'm not abandoning you for an office party, Angie!" Mila pulled a pillow beneath her chin. "There will be other office parties, but your wedding only happens once."

Angie pulled her legs up close to her chest and wrapped her arms around them. "You see a future with Zane? Marriage, even?"

"I'm expecting a holiday proposal."

"Really?"

"We have brunch with his parents once or twice a month. I get along with his sisters and he says his mom likes me, which is important, right?"

"Agreed."

"Our careers mesh. We both love living in the city—"

"You always talked about living in Colorado. You don't miss it?"

"I'll always miss Colorado. Those years were the best years of my life. But I live in New York now."

"With your job, you could live anywhere."

"Zane works with his father. The family financial business is based in the city. That dictates where we'll be living."

Angie rested her chin on top of her knees. "And he's a believer too?"

Mila paused. "Zane ... respects what I believe."

Angie's eyes narrowed. "What did you just say?"

"He respects—"

"Mila, you know that's not enough for you to marry this guy."

"What if I think it is? He believes in God."

"*Respecting what you believe* isn't the same—"

"It's enough for me."

"Why?"

"Respect is important in any marriage. We can build on it. He goes to church with me ... when I go..."

"And his 'sometimes' faith is enough? What if after you get married he stops going to church with you?"

Hours later as Mila lay awake, tucked under a heated blanket, staring at the ceiling of her bedroom, Angie's questions echoed in the darkness. Angie hadn't pretended to be satisfied with the *"we can build on it"* Mila had stammered out earlier. Mila had feigned tiredness and called it a night within ten minutes.

Now it was two-thirty in the morning, and sleep eluded her.

She loved Zane. Of course she did. Who wouldn't? He loved her. Marrying him was the right next step.

"God, you know I believe in You ..." Her incomplete whisper faded into the silence of the bedroom.

How was she supposed to finish that sentence? Belief was one thing. Trust was another. Ben and Angie and Charles had always seemed to trust God more easily than she did. Their belief had bolstered hers.

But life in New York had pushed God aside—allowed the doubts to run rampant. Not something she was proud of. But also not something that was a priority for Zane. At least not yet.

"God ... I just don't believe in happily ever afters."

She wanted to snatch the words back. What was she doing talking to God about fairy tales? She sounded like a young girl who wanted a prince to show up and whirl her around the ballroom. But her parents had proven how ridiculous those romantic ideals were when their marriage imploded.

She trusted Ben more than anyone in the world, which was why she wouldn't ruin their friendship. Friendship and falling in love were two very different things. Mixing the two together resulted in heartache for everyone involved— her parents' failed marriage taught her that.

She didn't want Zane to be her best friend. She had that with Ben. And Angie too, of course. Zane would be the best kind of husband. He was rock steady. Focused on his career. Financially stable. That was enough.

Mila picked up her phone and debated whether to send an *I miss you* text to Zane.

An overlooked text from Ben timestamped at midnight waited for her.

You'll be the prettiest Mrs. Claus the town of Chestnut has ever seen.

His words embraced her like a comfortable hug—one that she needed to shrug out of.

Mila turned onto her side. She'd made a choice years ago between falling in love with Ben Kendrick or saving their friendship. She'd chosen their friendship. Their friendship had survived both long distance and their disastrous attempt at dating. Ben was the best. But he just wasn't—couldn't be—her knight on a white horse.

She huffed a laugh. There was that ridiculous phrase again.

She was a grown woman who didn't need a knight, on or off a horse. She could take care of herself, which was one of the things Zane admired about her. She wasn't a needy female.

The almost-kiss between her and Ben in the hallway? There was no denying that tantalizing moment ... but best to think of it as some sort of glitch.

She needed to meet this plus-one Ruby woman. See if she was good enough for Ben Kendrick.

CHAPTER 7

Determined to reset things with Angie before she left for work at the high school, Mila dragged herself out of bed at six, despite her body's protests. No need for any more intense conversation, but they could start the day with a nice breakfast together. After a hot shower, she dressed in jeans and a soft red sweater for the forecasted snow and then prepped breakfast. Angie wandered into the kitchen half an hour later.

"What smells so good?"

"Pancakes. I used the rest of the mix. Or maybe the bacon lured you out of bed. There's a fresh pot of coffee too."

"What's the occasion?"

"Just pampering the bride to be." Mila motioned for Angie to sit at the table. "How many pancakes do you want to start with?"

"I'll take two, with two slices of bacon, please."

Mila served her friend a mug of hot coffee first, setting the cream and sugar next to the jar of Charles's honey, then set a plate with the requested meal in front of her. She filled a plate for herself and sat across the table from her. Angie clasped her hand and thanked God for their food.

"What will you do while I'm at work today?" Angie buttered her pancakes and topped them with honey.

"I have work too. And I need to ask Ben if he's had any luck with a photographer. I'll text him about that. I also finally talked to the bakery owner yesterday—Carla, right?—and told her we wanted to discuss a groom's cake. She said practically any time today would work for her."

"I can take a long lunch around eleven. We can meet there and finalize the dessert table. Do you think guests will be disappointed there isn't an actual wedding cake?"

"Angie, they'll get to choose from mini carrot cakes, mini fruit tarts, cheesecake, and macarons. People will love having a selection."

"I hope so. But there won't be a traditional cake cutting."

"At your wedding you make your own traditions. Your own memories." Mila added another dollop of cream to her coffee. "Can we also stop by the art gallery and talk to Ruby about the setup for the rehearsal dinner?"

"That's a good idea."

"What are your guest favors?"

"Um ... I haven't decided." Angie hid her face behind her hands.

"What? Angie, no."

"With everything going on, we overlooked that detail. We're doing small welcome bags at the hotel for out-of-town guests. I do know that."

"Well, that's always nice." Mila scanned the list she and Angie had created when she'd arrived, adding *welcome bags for out-of-town guests*. "What's included?"

"Water bottles, lip balm, gum, tissues, maybe a granola bar or two—things like that."

"We'll have to research options for guest favors. Something personal that reflects you and Charles." Mila stood. "You done?"

"Yes. Breakfast was delicious. Meet you at Carla's Bakery in a few hours."

After Angie left, Mila settled on the couch with her laptop and called Zane, only to be sent to his voicemail. Of course, it was two hours later in New York, which meant he was already caught up in the busyness of his work day.

"I love you and I just wanted to say I'm sorry I'll miss the office party." She pushed aside the memory of the moments with Ben last night. "We'll talk later."

The more apologies, the better, right?

She hung up and texted Ben.

> Did you find a replacement wedding photographer? Priority #1.

Give a man a chance.
Good morning to you too.

> Sorry. We don't have a lot of time.

It's at the top of my list. See you later.

All too soon and with not enough work accomplished, Mila bundled up to meet Angie. She'd found the gloves Ben gave her in her coat pockets, a reminder of his kindness.

It was nice to be able to walk and meet Angie, like how she walked to places in New York City—but much quieter and with fewer people. One of the things she missed about Colorado.

Angie waved at her outside a shop with a festive scene complete with reindeer and elves painted on the large front window under a striped awning. "Right on time."

"I was ready for a break." The mixed aroma of yeast and cinnamon teased Mila's nose once they entered the shop.

"Hi, Carla." Angie led the way to the cash register, where a woman waited, her brown hair threaded with a few gray highlights and pulled back in a casual ponytail. The display case was filled with cinnamon rolls, donuts, and plump gingerbread cookies.

"Angie, I was sorry to hear about your wedding coordinator—and your photographer."

"You just stay healthy, okay? No more disasters for me and this wedding." Angie motioned Mila forward. "This is Mila, one of my best friends. She's also my maid of honor."

"We talked on Tuesday." Carla's smile warmed her deep brown eyes behind her plum-colored oval glasses. "You've been to Chestnut before, right?"

"Yes, but it's been a while." Mila shook hands with the woman, whose red holiday apron was adorned with small silver jingle bells along the hem. "We want to double-check about the dessert table for the wedding, but Angie also wondered if she could order a groom's cake for Charles."

"If it's not too late." Angie offered Carla a quick smile.

"Depending on what you had in mind, I could probably do that for you."

"Something with an outdoorsy theme. You know how Charles is all about hiking and mountain biking and cross-country skiing."

"It's his and Ben's business, after all," Carla agreed.

"I also had an idea, thanks to those yummy-looking gingerbread cookies." Mila took a sample of a snickerdoodle cookie from the tray on the top of the glass case and savored the spicy nibble coated with a sprinkle of sugar and cinnamon. "What if you made a small gingerbread log cabin?

Something rustic, with skis or snowshoes outside and something like 'Newlywed Cottage' or 'Just Married' or even your names across the front door?"

"What an adorable idea!" Angie clasped her hands together. "And Charles loves gingerbread."

"I could probably do a something like that for you." Carla nodded. "Let me mull over some ideas. Come by next Tuesday and I'll show you what I've come up with. I'll also give you the final list of items for the dessert table for the reception."

"That sounds perfect, Carla." Mila shook her hand again. "Could I also buy two gingerbread men and two cinnamon rolls?"

"Checking out my work?" Carla winked.

"Not at all. I just can't resist the delectable aromas any longer. But I'll have to share these with Angie and some other friends, or I won't fit into my maid of honor dress."

"If you'd like some coffee, it's on the house." Carla motioned behind them where a table held carafes, creamer, and sugars. "I pick it up from the coffee shop each morning. You can fix yourselves to-go cups while I bag these for you."

"That's perfect. Thank you." Mila held up one hand. "Oh, could you add an extra cinnamon roll, please."

"Sure thing."

Moments later, Angie sipped her coffee as they strolled toward the art gallery. "You must really like cinnamon rolls."

"The extra one isn't for me." Mila motioned Angie to enter Eye of the Beholder first.

A bell chimed as they entered, as if to cue the Christmas music that played in the background. The front window showcased a few watercolors on easels, an angel sculpture, several pieces of pottery, and an arrangement of Christmas-themed stained glass, all displayed around a small Christmas tree decorated in white lights.

The walls of the gallery also highlighted artists' paintings, additional watercolors, as well as oils. One corner of the front room showcased pottery. Mila would have to spend time there and see if she could find something for her mother. A mid-size display case promised an intriguing selection of handmade silver and turquoise jewelry.

"Good morning." A tall woman appeared from the upstairs room dressed in flowing black pants, wedge-heeled boots, and a dark-green knit sweater. "Welcome to Eye of the Beholder—oh, Angie, it's you."

"Hi, Ruby." When Ruby reached the bottom of the stairs, Angie hugged her. "This is Mila, my maid of honor."

Ruby offered her hand to Mila. "Angie told me about you."

Mila shook her hand, then opted for a brief hug. "I hope you don't mind. I believe in hugs, and we're both friends of Angie's, and we'll be seeing a bit of each other—"

Ruby's laugh was warm. "I'm a hugger, too, but didn't want to be pushy."

"Mila wanted to see the area for the rehearsal dinner."

"This is a good time because the shop is quiet. The plan is to let people mingle down here for appetizers and then go upstairs for the buffet. Angie hired some of the kids from her school to serve. They earn volunteer hours with the honor society for doing community service." Ruby smiled. "Don't worry. She said they're reliable, and they know what to wear."

"That's so great that you're helping out some high schoolers." Mila turned a slow circle in the center of the gallery. "Who's catering the rehearsal dinner?"

"The Italian restaurant in town—they're under new management. And then the reception will be at Calidad, the Mexican restaurant owned by Noah. He's also a fantastic chef. It's become so popular that people come from Vail and Aspen and Denver to eat there."

Ruby led the way upstairs to the more open portion of the art gallery with sculptures positioned near the walls, as well as some larger Colorado photography montages arranged along the walls. "Food-Ease will set up while we're doing the run-through for the wedding."

"Will there be tables and chairs for people to sit?"

"Up here, yes, so people have the option to sit or to stand."

"Maybe we can find a few taller tables too where people can stand and put their cups or plates while they mingle and talk."

"That's a good idea."

"We can keep the décor simple, thanks to the beautiful artwork, but some flowers might be nice. Did Sybil mention that, Angie?"

"I don't think so ..."

"I'll contact the florist and ask her. The name's in the folder, right?"

"Buds and Blooms Limited."

"Right. And I'll call the caterer. You said the name was Foodies?"

"Food-Ease—as in *easy*. F-o-o-d-dash-E-a-s-e."

"That's fun."

The electronic bell chimed as someone else entered the shop.

Ruby moved toward the stairs, her gaze on the monitor positioned on the wall. "Excuse me, but I need to go greet my customers."

"No problem." Mila motioned around the area. "We'll just take one last look around, if that's okay."

After she left, Mila turned to Angie. "Is there anything else you can think of before we leave?"

"No. I'm just so glad you're here. You've remembered things I've forgotten. You're better than my wedding coordinator."

"Hardly. I'm just following through on things like Sybil would have."

"I can't wait to talk to my mom and Fiona and let them know what we're getting done."

"It's nice to have some extra time together, and everything will be settled when your family arrives for the rehearsal dinner." The paper bag rustled as they descended the stairs. "Oh! I forgot to give Ruby a cinnamon roll. Let's do that, and then it's on to the next thing on our list."

"If she's busy with a customer, we'll just leave it on her desk in the back room with a note telling her to have a great day."

"Ruby seems nice. And she's so pretty with a bit of a boho flair. I love her layered hairstyle and that sweater. I think she'd be good for Ben."

Angie grinned. "You mean *good enough*."

"I'm still deciding. It's going to take someone very special to be good enough for Ben."

The question was, how would Ruby feel about Ben and Mila's friendship? Would Mila need to step back so Ben could find happiness with another woman?

CHAPTER 8

It was the perfect night for the next step in Operation Kiss Mila Maxwell—the sleigh ride.

The air had a cold bite to it that demanded warm coats, hats, and gloves. Once they were situated in the bright red sleigh, Ben tucked one of his grandmother's quilts around Mila. Overhead, stars lit up the midnight-blue sky. A lone owl called out to them as the horses wended their way through the path in the forest. Their hooves *shusshed* on the packed snow, and the large brass bells on their halters jingled when they shook their heads.

"Angie will be so surprised with this sleigh ride after the rehearsal dinner." Beside him, Mila's words appeared as puffs of white clouds. "We just need to make certain she'll be warm enough. I'll double-check what she plans to wear that night. Maybe I can smuggle a pair of her warmer boots into the trunk of Charles's car."

"I'll ask Tim to put some extra blankets in the sleigh." Ben added that additional item to his mental checklist. "Maybe some of those little hand warmer packets to slip in their gloves."

"Good ideas. And please make sure Charles doesn't wear one of his crazy sweaters."

"Heard. No tinsel sweater for the rehearsal dinner. And this next part of the ride will help too."

"What?"

With a slight pull on the reins, Ben slowed the horses' easy steps as they entered a clearing among the trees. A small portable table was set up. On it was a camp stove with a metal pot, along with insulated cups, a ladle, and a bag of marshmallows.

Ben motioned ahead. "Would you like some hot chocolate?"

Mila clapped her gloved hands. Her laughter added a bit of background music to the woodsy setting. "What a perfect surprise, Ben. A sleigh ride and hot chocolate."

"Why don't you wait here while I bring it to you?"

"Oh, let's get out and walk around for just a few minutes."

"You won't get too cold?"

"I'll be all the happier to get back in the sleigh." Mila slid over and then paused with one leg still in the sleigh. "The horses won't wander off?"

"Tim told me they know the routine. I tie them to that tree marked with the red ribbon, and they'll be content while we enjoy our hot chocolate. I even brought along a couple of apple pieces for them to munch on."

Ben ladled the dark steamy liquid into insulated paper cups while Mila walked around the small site. "Normally, there are workers here to serve the hot chocolate. Someone set this up and watched over it until we got here. When they heard the horses' bells, they made themselves scarce right before we arrived."

"If they do that for Angie and Charles, it'll be more romantic." Mila added two marshmallows to her drink. "Want a couple?"

"What's hot chocolate without marshmallows?"

"I agree." Mila surveyed the surroundings. "I wonder if we can do anything more for Charles and Angie's sleigh ride?"

"Like what?"

"Instead of paper cups, have some cute holiday mugs for them to use. Maybe whipped cream in addition to marshmallows. Sprinkles. And cookies! We need cookies too."

"There'll be other sleigh rides that night—"

"But if Charles and Angie are the last one, which they might be because it's after the rehearsal dinner, then maybe ..."

"You want me to ask Tim, right?"

Mila tilted her head, her loose curls spread across her shoulders. "Would you, please? I'll supply all the extras."

And there was Mila's smile. The one he'd seen the first day he'd met her. It lit up her eyes and warmed him on the inside better than an entire pot of hot chocolate.

He'd told Mila "no" plenty of times. No, he wouldn't take her on a hike ever again dressed in nothing more than a T-shirt, jeans, and casual shoes. No, she shouldn't try to take twenty-two credit hours her second semester. No, he didn't like her dating the foreign exchange student who whispered who-knew-what to her in Italian.

No, he didn't agree they shouldn't date.

He'd lost that argument, but why would she take him seriously when he'd been sweating inside a pink bunny suit? And then he'd lost the argument again the next day, when he realized she was choosing their friendship over their romance—and why.

Tonight, and whenever she smiled at him like that, he'd say yes to just about any request.

Chilled moonlight filtered down through the trees as Ben ushered Mila back into the sleigh and tucked the quilt around her. "You wait here while I clean up our mess."

He tossed their trash in the nearby can, did a quick wipe down of the table, and placed a twenty-dollar bill under the bag of marshmallows. Then he untied horses and joined Mila in the sleigh.

"Goodnight! Thanks for everything!" He raised his voice and waved to the workers hidden nearby as the horses returned to the path. "You warm enough?"

Mila pulled the blanket tighter and moved closer. "I will be. I forgot how cold it is here."

This was nice. He should have asked Tim about the long way back.

Ben gave the reins a gentle shake, and the horses moved forward. "We agree on a romantic sleigh ride for Charles and Angie?"

"Yes. I love this. It's perfect, especially if we add those few extra touches."

"On it."

"Thank you, Ben."

"Happy to do it." He paused. "I've missed you, Mila."

She shifted so her head rested on his shoulder. "I've missed you too, Ben."

He stilled. Was the secret mission working?

"Sometimes I wish you didn't live all the way across the country."

There. He'd said it.

"It's funny you say that." Mila yawned. "I told Angie I miss Colorado ... my four years here were the best ..."

"I agree." He kept his words simple. Didn't dare say, *"Your four years here were the best years of my life too."*

"Things change." Her words were softer.

"Sometimes change is good. Look at Angie and Charles getting married after dating all that time."

"Oh ... they've dated forever ..."

"Only took them ten years. But now we're days from their wedding."

"Not everyone's as lucky as Angie ... and Charles ..."

"Not everyone, but a lot of people find their soulmates."

"If you say so ..."

After a few moments of silence, Ben took a deep breath and stepped off the invisible cliff that separated him and Mila.

"Do you ever think about what happened between us, Mila? Maybe when we dated in college, we were lucky enough to find each other? Not lucky. That God knew we were right for each other?"

Mila was silent, so Ben kept talking.

"I know we can't go back and have a do-over. We're different people now. And don't think I've forgotten about Zane."

Still no response.

"All I'm asking is if there's the possibility you'd consider giving us another chance. Especially before you commit to something permanent with Zane."

Silence.

"Mila?"

Ben twisted to the right just the slightest bit. The sweep of Mila's eyelashes against her skin confirmed his suspicion.

His best friend was so comfortable with him that she'd fallen asleep snuggled up against him while he'd bared his heart and dared to ask her to date him again.

Wasted words. Wasted hope.

He shifted so he could wrap his arm around Mila, the woman he loved. Let her sleep as he held her close.

Not the Hallmark end to the night he'd imagined.

A mission gone bad.

Then again, it wasn't a no either.

And there was still the town's Christmas Festival. Anything could happen on Saturday.

CHAPTER 9

Chestnut knew how to do Christmas. Mila was caught up in all the holiday hoopla—and here she was, front and center in all the festivities.

In this town, Santa and Mrs. Claus didn't arrive in a sleigh. No, they rode on top of the town's antique fire engine driven by a grinning fireman—decked out in all the gear—who made sure the horns and lights blared as they made their way through the town.

Seated beside Ben, Mila gritted her teeth, smiled, and waved at the crowd of townspeople and visitors assembled along the sidewalks on both sides of the main street. Everyone was bundled up in winter coats, hats, and scarves, but the cold didn't stop the celebration.

"You didn't tell me about this part, Kendrick."

"Forgot."

"Sure you did."

"Keep smiling, Maxwell. Don't get your apron twisted. It's for the kids."

And off Ben went, waving and ho-ho-ho-ing like a pro. The new beard covered most of his face, his brown hair and beard hidden, while his hazel eyes twinkled just like the classic Christmas poem dictated.

Two hours later, she held court with jolly ol' Santa and doled out small candy canes to children who shared their wishes with Ben, as if he was the magical old man.

Her scalp itched underneath the curly white wig Ben had delivered last night along with a small pair of wire frame spectacles that slid down her nose no matter how many times she adjusted them. She'd perfected a nonstop juggling act. Rearrange her pillowy mid-section. Pull candy canes from her pockets. Push her silver wire frame glasses back into position on her nose. Sneak a Lemonhead. Repeat.

But it was for the kids who believed Christmas was wonderful.

Traditional music sounded through the town square. Vendors offered all types of food, from hot apple cider to sugar cookies to red and green popcorn balls. Shops were open, banners declaring specials for anyone who wanted to do a little holiday shopping. And tonight, the large tree at the end of town would be lit. Celebration was everywhere, woven together with laughter and neighbors greeting one another with nonstop calls of "Merry Christmas!"

No one suspected that Mrs. Claus was secretly a Scrooge.

"Come on. Time for a break." Ben stood and stretched.

"We get a break?"

"Don't you want one?"

"Absolutely! But what about the kids?"

"Spoken like the true Mrs. Claus." Ben pointed toward a trio of teens dressed like elves.

"They'll take over candy cane duty. We'll come back in fifteen minutes and do another two hours, and then we're done and can take off these fancy duds."

"Can we get something to drink?" Mila tucked her hands in her pockets to resist the urge to remove her wig and cap.

"Follow me." Ben led the way to a nearby vendor selling a variety of drinks. "What sounds good? Hot cider? Or something cold?"

"Just water. This outfit is a lot warmer than I expected."

"Agreed." He held up two fingers. "Two waters, please."

"On the house, Santa."

"Thanks, Dylan."

Mila smiled her gratitude as she twisted off the bottle cap and gulped down some water. Ah, relief.

"What do you think of Chestnut's Christmas Festival?"

"The town goes all out, doesn't it?"

"We love all the holidays. You should see Fourth of July. But I have to say, we do Christmas especially well."

Mila would rather be home in her regular clothes, snuggled under a blanket with a pillow behind her head, which was where all pillows should be. She'd watch a movie. Anything but a Christmas movie.

"Ready to finish our shift as the Clauses?"

"Want an honest answer?" Mrs. Claus—not that there was a real one—wouldn't whine.

"Not gonna abandon me now, are you, Maxwell?"

"I'm not a quitter, Kendrick, you know that. I do wish I had my old hiking boots today."

"Your what?"

"My boots. The ones you bought me after our first hike."

"You still have those things?"

"Of course. That purchase was my first step to becoming a real outdoorswoman."

"No pun intended, right?"

"What?" Mila had to laugh at the unintended joke. "Forget I said that."

"It's time for you to get a new pair of boots." Ben waved at different people as they wove their way through the crowds. Everyone knew him—and he knew everyone.

"I don't have a lot of time for hikes in New York."

"Then why do you keep them?"

"Sentimental, I guess."

"About boots? And you say you're not the romantic one." Ben glanced at his watch. "Only two hours left. You ready?"

Mila meant it when she said yes. In a few moments, Ben would become Santa again and dispense magical good cheer in a store-bought outfit and convince more than a few of the kids he lived at the North Pole. He was so good with the children. Didn't matter if he was talking eye to eye with a kindergartner, holding a baby, or joking with a group of middle schoolers.

He'd always talked about wanting a big family. Was that still true? There was no doubt he'd be a wonderful dad, no Santa Claus outfit needed.

At last, her apron pockets were empty, the last candy cane doled out to a tired toddler nestled against his mom's shoulder. Not even a piece of sour candy left. Mila's face felt frozen in a permanent smile, and the icy wind hadn't helped. Her voiced rasped from repeating "Merry Christmas" for hours. She could only hope she'd sounded like a cheerful old lady. Someone who loved Santa. Who loved Christmas.

Ben's laughter had never wavered in its merriment, and his eyes still glinted beneath his Santa's hat.

As the last family wandered off, Mila leaned against him with a groan. "Aren't you tired?"

"Exhausted."

"Then let's go get our normal clothes at the fire station and get out of these outfits." She tugged at his beard.

He stepped back with a shake of his head. "We can't do that!"

"Why not? Our work here is done."

"But the children are everywhere. We can't stop being Santa and Mrs. Claus—"

"Oh, come on, Ben, it's not like those kids believe we're really—"

"Some of them do. And I'm not going to break their hearts."

"Ben." She stared at him. Waited for him to grin and pull off his beard.

Nothing.

"Fine. I'll get my clothes and go back to Angie's to change."

Ben grabbed her hand before she took two steps. "But we haven't done anything today."

"What? We've just spent hours doling out Christmas cheer and candy canes."

"You haven't really seen the festival. Where's your Christmas spirit?"

Mila stomped her foot, not that he could see it underneath all the layers of fabric and pillows. "I'm dressed up in red velvet with a hundred pounds of feathers stuffed under my apron. I'm wearing a wig that makes me want to scratch my head for a half hour and then wash my hair at least three times! And you want to know where my Christmas spirit is?"

"Wrong question ..."

She huffed a breath and marched past him.

"I know just what you need." Ben kept pace with her.

"Not listening."

"Come on, Mila, it'll be fun."

"Getting out of these clothes will be fun. Taking off this wig. Fun. Showering? Pure bliss."

Ben grabbed her hand again. "Trust me, it'll be a blast. Then I promise, you can go home, and I'll get you whatever you want for dinner."

Mila stopped. "Whatever I want?"

"Yep. I'll even cook for all of us—you, me, Charles, Angie—"

"What if I want a grilled cheese sandwich?"

"You got it."

"I mean an ooey-gooey grilled cheese sandwich. All the cheese."

"Understood."

"And tomato soup."

"That too."

"And a hot fudge sundae."

"Yep."

A good carb overload was the perfect end to this day. "All right. What are we doing?"

"Follow me." Beneath his beard, Ben's grin was wicked. What was Santa Baby planning?

Too late to back out now. And how bad could it be?

As he led her up the steep hill twenty minutes later, Mila had to admit this was much worse than she'd imagined.

"Ben, I'm not dressed for this kind of physical activity." Mila grabbed fistfuls of her skirt and hiked it up near her knees as she trudged through the snow up the hillside.

"What are you complaining about? I'm carrying both snow tubes." Ben didn't even sound winded as he led the way, one large black PVC tube under each arm.

"It's the least you could do after you talked me into this."

"This is just what we need. Consider it stress relief." As he spoke, two teens slid down the middle of the steep slope, one careening to the left, one turned backward, as their laughter trailed behind them. "See? Told you."

"Neither of them is in costumes."

"Quit grumbling, Millie. We're almost to the top."

"People are pointing at us, Benjie."

"Not every day you get to see Santa and the missus go tubing." Ben's laughter filled the air. "I think we're making history here. Maybe we'll end up in the paper."

"Perfect. My five minutes of fame will be as a snow-tubing Mrs. Claus."

When they reached the top, the small crowd applauded and cheered them on as they positioned their tubes side by side. Ben took her hand and helped Mila settle into the giant tube, waiting while she rearranged her billowing skirt and made sure her wig and mobcap were secure. A teen in a bright orange vest held her snow tube still, while Ben settled beside her in his.

"Give me a little head start, okay?" Mila whispered with a wink.

"No fair, wife."

"Ho ho ho to you, Santa Ba-beee—" Mila's taunt ended in a shrill scream when the lanky teen gave her a shove over the edge of the hill.

For a moment she was airborne, and her heart seemed to match the upward motion of her body. Then she settled back on the ground with a thud that caused her white curls to shift as her tube skidded down the snow-covered hill. Giggles rippled from her, and she glanced over her shoulder.

Ben slid toward her, his body sideways in the big black tube. The gathered crowd cheered as he belly-laughed, one hand gripping the side of his snow tube as he waved wildly with his other hand.

Ben was right. This was fun.

And it was going to be even more fun when she beat him to the bottom of the hill.

As they neared the finish line—had they declared this a race?—Ben's tube knocked into hers just as they hit an icy patch and turned her around. They both spun out of control. Mila launched out of her tube, and then they tumbled into a pile of snow, Mila on top of Ben.

Laughter and cries of "Bravo" and "Go again!" surrounded them.

"You okay there?" Ben stared up at her, his arms wrapped around her, white beard askew.

"I think so." Mila repositioned his fake beard. "I lost my wig."

"You look beautiful."

"Flatterer." She pressed her hands against his chest.

"I mean it." He caressed the side of her face with his fingertips. "You've always been the most beautiful woman to me."

His words cued the opening notes of "All I Want for Christmas Is You" and the emotion darkening Ben's hazel eyes lured Mila closer.

One kiss. What was wrong with one kiss?

"Mila!" A voice rose above the cheers.

Wait ... who was that?

"Mila!" Footsteps crunched through the snow. "Are you okay?"

She forced herself to look away from Ben even as he pulled her closer.

"Zane?"

Ben tensed beneath her and the soft notes jolted to a stop.

"What ... what are you doing here?"

She needed to rephrase that.

"I came to Chestnut to surprise you." Zane opened his arms wide, his smile twisted. "Surprise."

Mila discovered a whole new level of awkwardness as both her long skirt and Ben's arms and legs hindered her attempts to stand.

"Stop. Helping." Mila froze in place. "*Please.*"

Ben collapsed back into the snow. "Fine."

When Zane offered her a hand, she took it and stepped over Ben. "Sorry."

"No problem." Ben shoved to his feet and brushed snow off his outfit.

Mila adjusted her ensemble. Pillow. Skirt. The mobcap and wig were somewhere on the side of the hill. "Zane, I'm so surprised to see you."

"That was the plan." Zane's reply was stiff. No hug. No kiss.

Just as she started to introduce Ben, Angie and Charles showed up. Angie danced a silly jig. "Santa and Mrs. Claus have never snow-tubed during the Christmas Festival! You two are the talk of the town!"

Charles slapped Ben on the back. "Sounds like you might make the front page of the newspaper tomorrow."

Mila groaned. "Please say you're kidding."

"I bet we can get copies of some of the photos—"

Time for introductions.

Mila stepped closer to Zane and linked their arms. Now at least they looked like a couple. An odd couple, to be sure. "Angie, Charles, um, look who showed up to surprise me. Zane." She ended the announcement with an awkward *Ta-da!* flourish.

Angie's gaze bounced from Zane to Mila. "This is Zane?"

"Yes."

"I should have recognized you from the photos Mila shared. Welcome to Chestnut." Just as Angie stuck her hand out, Charles did the same with a "Nice to meet you" so Zane's attempt to take Angie's hand became a tangled three-way handshake.

"And this is Ben. You've heard me talk about Ben. And Angie. And Charles." Mila pointed to her friends one at a time. "The wedding."

"Yes. Nice to meet you all at last."

Zane and Ben gave each other a quick nod.

"So you decided to come see the Christmas Festival?" Angie shifted closer to Charles.

"I came to see Mila. Found out about the festival when I arrived."

What was wrong with Zane? Where was the easygoing man she knew and loved?

"Well then, let me show you around." Mila scanned the other three. "You want to join us?"

"That's okay." Angie spoke first. "You two have fun. Stop by the townhouse later and we can visit for a while."

"We just might do that." Mila patted Zane's arm.

If Zane thawed out and relaxed.

Mila was caught in Chestnut's annual winter wonderland, lit by thousands of white twinkly lights, with nonstop holiday music that included a troupe of carolers who wended their way through the festive crowd of townspeople and tourists.

And with Zane.

Zane—who stuck to schedules and routines—had been spontaneous and flown cross-country from New York. She should be elated.

But it was more like she'd been tossed into a giant snow globe.

Shake and tilt. Shake and tilt.

"That was quaint." Zane's words were tight. Dismissive.

"What?" Mila slowed her steps as they strolled through the main part of town, holding hands. Her gloves—Ben's gloves—shielded her skin from Zane's touch. "You didn't like the Christmas tree lighting?"

"It certainly can't rival the tree in Rockefeller Center."

"Chestnut isn't trying to compete with that—or anything else. This is our town's tradition."

"Your town's?"

"*The town's tradition*. Although I love Colorado like I'm a native, I realize I'm not."

"Are you staying in that getup all night?"

Mila retightened the apron as the skirt now dragged on the ground around her feet after Angie had offered to take the pillow back to the townhome. "I need to go back to

Angie's to change, and then you'll have a chance to get to know Angie and Charles and B—"

Zane pulled her to a stop. "Can we talk first, please?"

"You're not ready for me to change out of my not-so-secret identity?"

No laughter met her attempted joke.

"I flew to Colorado because I missed you and wanted to see you. Not to walk around a Christmas festival. Not to spend time with your friends." He motioned to a nearby bench. "Let's sit down for a minute."

Mila gathered her skirt around her feet, thankful that Angie had offered to pick up the clothes she'd left at the firehouse and then gave Mila her down coat before she and Charles left. "Is something wrong?"

"My mom and sisters told me that showing up like this would be romantic." Zane spoke the words almost to himself, punctuated with a quiet laugh.

"Zane, I'm sorry—"

"Come back to Denver with me tonight." His request cut her off.

"What?"

Zane moved closer as he took her hand. "I have a ticket for you to fly back to New York with me in the morning. You can be there for the office party on Tuesday and then fly back here the next morning."

"Zane, I can't do that." Mila twisted the velvet material of her dress between her fingers. "I have so much to do with work and Angie's wedding—"

"You had time to play Mrs. Claus and go snow tubing."

"I was helping Ben. His parents usually play Santa and Mrs. Claus but they couldn't this year—"

"It looked to me like you were going to kiss the guy you keep telling me is merely your best friend."

Zane's accusation iced her heart. He'd seen ... *something* between her and Ben. But nothing had happened.

"I wasn't kissing Ben Kendrick." That was the truth. "Our snow tubes collided, and we fell into one another."

"I saw the whole thing, Mila. I saw how that guy looked at you."

"You're obviously misinterpreting whatever you saw. Ben and I are friends. Nothing more." Mila refused to look away from Zane. Didn't even blink. "I'm in love with you. Not Ben."

"Then come back with me to New York."

"What?" Mila pulled her hand away. "Is that somehow going to prove I love you?"

Zane gave a muffled groan. "I'm not saying that."

"That's what it sounded like."

"Don't twist what my words—"

"Don't tell me that I was going to kiss someone when I wasn't." Mila stood and turned away from Zane.

"Now you're going to walk away from me?"

Mila faced him again. Flexed her hands that had curled into fists. "I'm sorry. Would you please come back to Angie's with me?"

Zane stood. "I have an early flight tomorrow."

Mila's shoulders sagged. "It's not that late, Zane."

"I have to drive back to Denver tonight."

They stared at one another as people moved to their left and right.

"You'll be back for the wedding?"

"Of course." Zane stuffed his hands in his coat pockets. "I'm looking forward to it."

Somehow, Mila didn't believe him.

"Goodbye, Mila." Zane turned away without even a kiss.

She'd learned at thirteen not to drag out goodbyes. Not to cry. It didn't change anything.

"Have a safe flight."

She held her voice steady. It was okay. There'd been another Christmas season that was all tangled up in choices like a snarled string of holiday lights. When the festive music had faded and the lights dimmed. That's when she'd given up on make believe and Santa Claus and happily ever after.

CHAPTER 10

The Grinch was in town and his name was Zane Halverson.

Ben prowled Angie's townhouse, his game pieces ignored on the Catan board. "It's been more than two hours. What do you think they're doing?"

"Zane's her boyfriend." Angie offered a smile. "They're probably holding hands, enjoying the lights, talking—"

"You really think that guy flew out here to see the lights?"

Angie sat on the couch next to Charles, who wore a *Star Wars*–themed Christmas sweater. "He came to see Mila. And now she wants to show him the town."

"They could have gone back to his hotel." This from Charles.

"Thanks for that."

"I'm just saying—"

"Am I missing something here?" Angie looked back and forth between Charles and Ben.

"No. You're not missing a thing." Ben took another circle around the living room.

"Next time you pass the coffee table, you want to take your turn? This game doesn't require ten-minute pauses."

Before Ben could respond, the front door opened, and Mila slipped inside.

Alone.

Angie rose to face Mila. "Where's Zane? I hoped he'd come back with you."

Mila's shoulders shifted under the Mrs. Claus dress she still wore, her hair disheveled around her shoulders. "Um, no. He's on his way back to Denver. Early flight."

"He's going back to New York so soon?"

"Yeah." Mila's voice seemed to fade more with each word.

What kind of guy flew to Colorado and stayed for less than twenty-four hours?

But before Ben could ask the question—any question— Mila moved past them.

"I'm exhausted. Handing out candy canes as Mrs. Claus is a tough gig. G'nite, everyone." Mila disappeared up the stairs, the red skirt trailing behind her.

Angie moved to follow. "I'm going with Mila."

Charles put a hand on her arm to stop her. "Angie, she just said she's exhausted."

"That doesn't mean she wants to be alone. Make sure everything's locked up when you leave."

"Sure thing." He stopped Angie for a brief kiss and an exchange of "I love you."

If only Ben could talk to Mila. He pulled out his phone to start a text. Stopped. *I'm sorry* seemed inadequate.

AH4UB

Not that he expected her to text back an AH4UM.

Five years ago, he'd smashed his ankle hotdogging on his snowboard. Mila had shown up the day of surgery with a ridiculous "snowboarder bear" all bandaged up from his own imaginary surgery, and then she'd stayed a week with Angie to ensure Ben followed his doctor's orders. Made batches of soup and stored portions in his freezer. Kept him on track with his meds. Played endless rounds of Crazy Eights and video games with him. Watched all the movies he liked, even though she wasn't a fan of suspense.

He couldn't buy a stuffed bear to fix Mila's disappointment. She and Zane would have to figure things out for themselves.

"This is great, right?" Charles clapped him on the back before he sat back on the couch.

"That Zane's going back to New York? How so?"

"The way I see it, he just made Operation Kiss Mila Maxwell a whole lot easier."

"They're still dating, Charles."

His friend started clearing away game pieces. "The guy showed up. Was here a few hours. And now, from the looks of it, there's trouble in paradise. Pardon the cliché. Make your move."

"Make my move." Ben stood in front of him. "Since when are you a romance expert?"

Charles sat back with his hands raised. "This is all Angie, not me."

"I don't know what to think." Ben rubbed the back of his neck. "There have been a couple of times when Mila seemed ready to ... when I thought if I kissed her ... Never mind."

"This is good."

"This is a ridiculous conversation."

"Just remember she and Zane need to break up at some point."

"I don't want to be the cause of Zane and Mila's breakup."

Charles removed his glasses and rubbed his eyes. "You might have to be. Mila has to realize she loves you, not Zane."

"It would be better if she breaks up with him, right?"

"What are you two talking about?"

Ben jerked around. Mila stood at the top of the stairs dressed in a heather gray Colorado sweatshirt and flannel pajama bottoms.

"You're still up."

"I'm tired." She advanced down the stairs, Angie behind her. "But I'm also hungry. Angie said you guys picked up takeout from Calidad."

"We ordered plenty, just in case you and Zane came by." Ben moved toward the kitchen.

"I'll eat his portion." Charles raised his hand.

As Mila got closer, tear stains were evident on her face, which was clean of all makeup. "Zane and I didn't break up, you know."

"That's good." His mom would wash his mouth out with soap for such a straight up lie. He risked putting an arm around her, not surprised when Mila remained as stiff as when he'd tried to embrace her when she'd broken up with him. "I'm sorry he upset you."

A moment later, she relaxed. Sniffled. "Thank you."

What now? "Anyone up for a good Christmas movie while Mila eats? Maybe *Die Hard*?"

She pushed away from him with a groan. "How many times do I have to tell you *Die Hard* is not a Christmas movie?" She poked his chest. "And don't tell me that Bruce Willis said it is."

At least she looked more ready to argue with him than to cry. "How about *Elf* or *Klaus*?"

"Can we watch anything but a Christmas movie?" Mila brushed away the remnants of tears on her face. "Come on, Kendrick, keep a weepy woman company?"

"You don't have to ask twice, Maxwell, especially if you share those leftovers."

"Hear, hear." Charles's cheer made both Angie and Mila laugh.

The mood had shifted. They were friends. Best friends. He'd leave it at that for now. And hope for more.

You awake, Ben?

Yep. You?

Obvi. I'm texting you.

How ya be?

Been better.

Want to FaceTime?

NO! I'm not a pretty crier.

...

Don't say it, Ben.

Say what?

That Zane isn't worth crying over.

Can't stop me from thinking it.

> I love him, Ben. That doesn't change just because
> we had a fight. We'll figure things out.

...

Want to go snowshoeing this morning?

> Thanks but no. I'm going to try to sleep.
> Angie wants me to go to church with them.
> See where the wedding will be.
> They're using some of the church's Christmas
> decorations for the wedding.

I'll let you try and sleep then.
Praying for you.

> Thanks, Ben.

AH4UB

> I know. <3

Mila rolled over onto her side and set her phone on the charging stand before she pulled the blankets up to her shoulders again.

Nothing from Zane. Not that she'd called or texted him. She didn't know what to say.

Zane had hinted about a proposal. Had he already bought her an engagement ring? After tonight and how she chose Angie over him, would he return it?

She pulled the blankets closer as a shiver ran down her body. Why couldn't she just cry herself to sleep? It was two o'clock and all she'd done was replay all the things Zane had said—and all the things she'd wished she'd said.

Now she lay awake and recalled how she and Zane met at a fundraiser auction when they bid on the same New York City Excursions basket that included the Statue of Liberty and Ellis Island Ferry ride, the 9/11 Memorial and Museum, and the Empire State Building with skip-the-line tickets. Zane had won the basket and then afterward invited her to join him on the excursions.

"But I don't know you—" Mila couldn't help but laugh at the handsome man in a tuxedo who stood in front of her when she tried to leave.

"Mrs. Smythe, would you please introduce me to this young lady as more than paddle number three hundred seventy-five?"

One of the chairwomen of the event had been all too happy to oblige. Introductions made, and assured of Zane's impeccable reputation, Mila accepted his invitation. From that day on, they'd dated steadily.

Until today.

No. Until last night when Zane had wanted her to choose between him and Angie and then questioned her friendship with Ben.

Mila threw back the covers. She needed the familiar comfort of Ben's hoodie, which she'd left in her closet back in New York. She'd never fall asleep without it. She might as well go downstairs and indulge in the immediate caloric comfort of a mug of hot chocolate.

As she descended the stairs to the darkened living room, she switched on the hallway light.

"Mila?" Something ... *someone* shifted on the couch and then eased to a sitting position.

Ben?

"What are you doing here?"

"Just decided to bunk on the couch for the night ... you know ..." He raked his fingers through his messy hair, his flannel shirt rumpled.

"Benton Kendrick, are you keeping an eye on me?"

"I was sleepy after all the Mexican food and watching the movie. I sent Charles home—"

He expected her to believe that? "Excuses, excuses."

"Fine. I was worried about you, and Angie said I could bunk on the couch."

Ben tugged at the blanket wrapped around his body. "Did you need something?"

"Hot chocolate sounded good."

"Say no more. Sit right here"—he shoved his blankets away—"and I'll turn on the fake fire and fix you a cup, complete with marshmallows."

Mila managed not to cry while Ben fixed their drinks, thankful for her self-control when they sat side by side on the couch. Now was as good a time as any. "Ben, I have a confession to make."

"A confession, huh?"

"Remember that old hoodie you used to wear?"

"My favorite hoodie that I loaned you and then you lost it?"

"I-I have it."

"What?" Ben's face was all exaggerated shock. "You *stole* my hoodie?"

"I didn't steal it. Not exactly." Mila shifted and met his gaze. "I didn't realize I had it in all my stuff when we graduated. I found it in a box when I unpacked and yes, awful friend that I am, I kept it. It's followed me from Kansas to New York. I wear it whenever I-I'm lonely or sad or homesick for Colorado."

Ben rested his hand on hers. "You've had the hoodie this long. It's yours now."

"Thanks, Ben. You've always been the person I trust the most." She rested her head on his shoulder. "I wished I had your hoodie tonight, but having you here to talk to is better."

"Well, thanks for that." His chuckle was low. Familiar.

"I can't figure it out. Why doesn't Zane understand helping Angie is more important than his office party ..." She pressed her lips together to cut off the rest of her words.

She would not cry any more tonight.

"Is that why he showed up today?"

"Yes. I mean, he said he missed me. And his mom and his sisters thought showing up here was romantic." Mila shifted against Ben, who placed his arm around her shoulders. "He said I'd only be gone a few days. When I told him I couldn't because I'm juggling too many work projects along with the wedding stuff, he wondered why I was playing around at the Christmas Festival."

She would not mention that Zane thought she was going to kiss Ben.

Because Zane was right.

She needed to forget those brief moments in Ben's arms. Find some way to stop the romantic Christmas music that played when he was near.

"He probably already regrets that he left—"

"He probably regrets that he came to Colorado."

Ben squeezed her shoulders. "Let me finish, will you? He probably regrets that he left with things like they are between you."

"Thank you. It helps that you're here. Back in New York, I'd be all alone in my apartment."

"Wearing my hoodie."

Mila laughed. "Hey! You said it's mine."

"True." He retrieved a pack of cards off the table beside the couch. "How about I beat you at a few rounds of Crazy Eights?"

"You're on, but first I'm breaking into Angie's stash of Christmas cookies."

"Living a dangerous life there, Maxwell."

"You know it, Kendrick."

Cookies and a game of cards were a nice distraction. Somehow, after a few hours' sleep, she'd find hope again and start over.

CHAPTER 11

Heartache was not the best frame of mind for planning a wedding.

Mila sat on her bed and stared at her phone. How was it already Tuesday morning, three days after Zane's surprise visit to Chestnut—and his abrupt departure? Tonight was his office Christmas party. She'd texted Zane Sunday morning when he flew back to New York. He hadn't texted back or called, and she'd allowed the silence to stretch across both the geographic and emotional miles between them.

She needed to talk to someone.

Not Angie, who had enough to deal with between work and her wedding.

Not Ben, who somehow muddled her thoughts about Zane.

Mila tapped speed dial, ready for some answers.

"Mila! I'm so glad you called."

"Hi, Mom. Are you busy?" Mila's bare feet hung over the edge of the bed.

"Never too busy to talk to you." Her mom's voice was so like her own. "I'm just making a grocery list. How are things in Colorado?"

She could say fine, or she could get right to the point. "Mom, this is going to come out of nowhere, but can I ask you something about when Dad left?"

Her mother didn't answer for a few moments. Then—"You're right. I wasn't expecting that."

"So you'll answer my question?"

"Honestly, Mila, I've waited years for you to ask me questions about the divorce. Most kids do."

Mila swung her legs up onto the bed and lay back against the pillows. "I've had them, but I thought it would be hard for you to talk about what happened."

"Honey, the divorce was hard for both of us. When your dad walked out, it broke my marriage, but it also broke our family."

Mila didn't want to go into all of that. Onto the question. "You don't think it's smart to marry your best friend, right?"

"That's your question?"

"Yes. I think I know the answer—"

"Wait." Her mom stopped her. "Why do you think I'm against best friends getting married?"

"About six months into the separation, I heard you crying on the phone with one of your friends. You said something about how Dad was your best friend, and you wished you'd never married him." Mila pulled one of the pillows from behind her and hugged it. "That's when I learned the truth about marrying your best friend."

"Mila." Her name was a plea. "Oh, I wish we'd talked about this back then. Our marriage didn't end *because we were best friends*. The divorce happened because your dad cheated on me. And you're old enough now for me to tell you that the last time—the time you know about—wasn't the first time your dad cheated."

"What?"

"I'm sorry if that's a shock, but I don't think you've had your dad up on a pedestal in years."

"True."

"So yes, I said those things, but I still believe marrying your best friend is a good idea."

"But he broke your heart, Mom."

"Yes, because he'd been my best friend for so many years and that made the affairs even more heartbreaking. But love is a risk. That's the truth, although people label it a cliché." Her mom sighed. "But you know all about trust and risk because you love Zane."

"Yes." Mila tossed the pillow aside. "Thanks, Mom. This helps a lot."

"Can I just say I always liked Ben Kendrick, even though you two only dated for a little while?"

Where was this coming from?

"Mom! Ben and I are just friends."

"My point exactly." There was the hint of a smile in her mom's words.

"I'll call soon. Love you."

Mila disconnected the call, tossed her phone next to the pillow, and fought the urge to roll to her side and go back to sleep.

Why was she more confused after talking to her mom? What now?

She forced herself to stand. She wasn't a quitter.

It was time to start the day. Her computer calendar was still as colorful as one of Charles's holiday sweaters and the wedding checklist also demanded her attention.

"But I still believe marrying your best friend is a good idea."

Her mom's words echoed in her mind.

Mila fisted her hands. "Sorry, Mom. I never said I agreed with you. I can't."

Caffeine scented the air as Mila's steps sounded on the stairs. Just before she walked into the kitchen, Mila straightened her shoulders and pasted such a wide smile on her face that the corners of her mouth hurt. No need for Angie to think she regretted being here. She'd made her decision. Zane had made his.

Angie poured herself a cup of coffee, then hovered the pot over a red mug painted with a sprig of holly and poured until Mila nodded for her to stop. "I know, you'll dilute this with a ridiculous amount of cream. How are you? I heard you get up around one o'clock—"

"Oh, I'm sorry ..."

"It's fine, Mila. I know you're hurting."

She wouldn't deny it.

Mila sat across from Angie at the kitchen table. "Do you know how ridiculous I looked, standing in the center of town by myself Saturday night after Zane left while everyone else celebrated Christmas?" The words spilled out as fast and unstoppable as if she'd tipped over her cup of coffee so the hot liquid poured over the side of the table and stained the floor.

"I wished you'd called. I would have come and picked you up."

"No, there was something almost laughable about walking through town in my costume. An abandoned Mrs. Claus. How symbolic."

"You still haven't talked to Zane?"

"He hasn't called or texted ... I didn't expect this to happen."

"Mila, I've told you—"

Mila held up her hand. "I *want* to be here. No regrets."

"None?"

"None."

Except maybe that'd she'd ever said yes to that first date with Zane. Or that she'd ever believed they'd create their own happy ending.

She might as well believe Ben was Santa.

"Enough about me. It's too early in the morning to talk about this, especially after we talked about it too late last night." Mila ran her fingers through her tangled hair. Gave her head a shake, as if she could clear her thoughts. "We've got less than two weeks to the wedding. Time to check our list—and please, nothing funny about checking it twice. I'm so over the jolly old man."

"I wasn't going to—"

"Oh yes you were."

"Guilty." Angie shrugged beneath a T-shirt that was bejeweled with the word *BRIDE*.

"You don't have to go into work until this afternoon. Let's focus on your wedding." Mila retrieved a banana from a bowl on the counter and peeled it. "We never finalized guest favors for the wedding reception."

Angie scrunched up her face. "You're right."

Mila huffed at a strand of hair that had fallen in front of her eyes. "Well, my not sleeping isn't all bad, because I had an idea. You know how Charles sells some of his honey from his beekeeping operation in his and Ben's shop?"

"Keep talking."

"Does Charles have enough to make gifts for your guests? We could order tiny individual jars and make labels that say 'Meant to Bee Mine' and add your initials and the wedding date. Or keep it simple and just do your initials and the date. And then add thin silver and blue ribbons to coordinate with your wedding colors."

"I love this idea! It's personal, and who doesn't like honey?" Angie bounced in her chair. "Charles has a good supply of honey because he had an excellent year with his beekeeping, but if we need more, he could ask some of the other local beekeepers to contribute."

"Great. We're going into town today anyway to talk to Carla about the groom's cake, so we can stop by the shop and talk to Charles."

"I'll text him your idea." Angie set aside her coffee and moved toward the fridge. "Do you want anything else to eat?"

"I'm good." Mila opened the calendar on her phone. "Your parents and sister arrive next Wednesday, and we'll have our spa day on Thursday—a belated bachelorette party."

"No one invites their mother to their bachelorette party."

"We'll just call it a spa day, and maybe I can take you out to dinner one night before they get here."

"Can we look at the church soon, so you can see how it's decorated?"

Mila sighed. "Thank you for letting me sleep in on Sunday—"

"It's fine, Mila. Ben told us you were up late."

"I'll call and see if we can stop by one day this week. I don't know if we can add anything to the flower order at this late date." Mila scanned the dates. "Maybe we could stop by the church this Thursday over your lunch hour?"

"Perfect."

"What are the guys doing while we're getting pampered?"

"They're going snowshoeing."

"Sounds fun. But I like our plan for the day much better."

"Oh, me too. I'm all for Charles having fun, but what can happen when they're basically walking through the woods, right?"

"Angie, you've got to relax. Just because you dreamed Charles broke his leg doesn't mean anything bad is going to happen to him before the wedding."

"You say this to the woman who's already lost her wedding coordinator—not that I'm complaining about Sybil's dilemma—and whose photographer broke her wrist." Angie slid a bagel into the toaster oven and closed the door with a metallic clang. "Forgive me if I'm a little paranoid."

"You forget your husband-to-be co-owns an outdoor shop."

"I don't mind when he's handing out gear for other people to go on their adventures in the mountains. But until our wedding is over, I'd prefer he play it safe."

"The man could still marry you with a broken leg—"

Angie whirled around to face her. "Don't say it!"

"I mean—"

"Don't. Say. It."

Mila raised her hands as she backed out of the kitchen. "I'm going to shower and get some work done. Let me know when you're ready to go into town.

Good morning.

Sleep okay?

I'm fine.

You didn't answer my question.

Q4U: you're just snowshoeing with Charles next Thursday? Nothing else planned?

Nope. Well, except going somewhere to eat. His dad and cousin are coming with us. We'll probably get lunch somewhere.

Your job is to keep Charles safe.

We're snowshoeing. What could happen?

Angie's still freaked about Charles getting hurt.

Fine. I'll be the best man and bodyguard.

Thanks. We'll be by later.

The stop by the bakery was quick. Carla showed them her rough sketch for the groom's cake and confirmed what time she'd deliver it and the desserts to the Mexican restaurant for the reception. They agreed on a quick stop at Chestnut's Roasting for coffee and ran into, of all people, Ruby.

"How are the wedding plans going?"

Mila shook the container marked cream and then poured a generous portion into her to-go cup. "Today is all about finalizing things as much as possible."

"Mila had a great idea to give away small jars of Charles's honey as guest favors at the reception."

"I love that."

Angie tucked several napkins in her coat pocket. "We just need to order bottles and labels and print them off—"

"Please let me do this for you, Angie. I'd love to help in some way."

"The rehearsal dinner is in your shop!"

"It's so easy to provide the space." Ruby brushed aside the idea that hosting the rehearsal dinner was any problem with a *Pfffft*. "Please, let me do this. How many guests do you expect?"

"We invited one hundred. We tried to keep it smaller, but the list grew because we both live in Chestnut."

"I'll research this for you and let you know what I find before I order anything."

"Her colors are blue and silver. We thought we might add ribbons to the jars." Mila secured her lid on the cup. "And maybe labels with their initials and the date. But you're the artist, you might come up with something more creative."

"This will be fun."

"Thank you! And I think it's great that you're Ben's date for the wedding."

"Ben's such a nice guy." Ruby leaned in closer to Mila and Angie. "But if I'm honest, I've always had a thing for his brother Cole."

"Cole?"

"Forget I said anything, please." Ruby's face flushed pink. "He's so busy with the family's medical practice, and I don't think he'd even know my name if someone asked him."

"I won't say anything, but Cole's crazy not to notice you."

Ruby sipped her coffee and focused on Mila. "What about you? Will you stay in town after the wedding and spend Christmas with Ben and his family?"

The question was like a jolt of straight black coffee. Unwelcome and hard to swallow.

"Um, no. I fly back to New York the evening after the wedding." She and Zane had coordinated their tickets.

"That's too bad. We could plan something fun if you were here for the holidays."

Mila gripped her coffee with both hands as if it would hold her steady. "That's a nice thought, but life waits back in New York."

Work did.

And Zane. She hoped.

After a quick goodbye, Mila stopped just outside the coffee shop and scanned the street. "I know there's a beauty salon somewhere in this town ..."

"There's the C&D Salon. It's owned by two sisters. Why?"

"Do they take walk-ins?"

"Yes. Again, why?"

"I'm ready for a change." Mila looked left, then right. "Which way did you say?"

"I didn't. Are you sure you want to change your hair all of a sudden—and this soon before the wedding?"

"First, I'm thirty-two years old and you're not my mother. I can do what I want with my hair. Second, you're the bride, not me. No one will be looking at me."

"I'm not trying to tell you what to do, Mila, but I had to live with a 'why did I do this' haircut for six months. I don't want you to do the same thing."

"Tell me where the salon is."

"How about some therapy shopping?"

"I can waste my time wandering the wrong way, or you can save us both time and take me to the salon."

"Promise me no mermaid hair?"

"I promise."

At the salon, a woman in her mid-fifties approached. Her two-inch pink platform heels coordinated with her long nails and lipstick.

"Hi, Miss Dolly."

"Angie." She came in for an all-encompassing hug. "Your appointment isn't until the day of the wedding."

"I wanted to see if you had a walk-in for my friend Mila. She's my maid of honor."

"Happens I do. Had a no-show for a body wave, and things are slow at the funeral parlor, so I'm just washing towels."

Mila froze. "The funeral parlor?"

"It's a small town. My sister Charlene and I do the prep work, so to speak." Miss Dolly gave her a once-over. "What are you interested in?"

Mila removed her hat, and her hair tumbled over her shoulders.

"Oh, your hair is gorgeous."

"Cut it."

"Cut it?" Miss Dolly's eyes widened so her false eyelashes touched her eyebrows. "How short you thinking?"

"To my shoulders."

"That will be a good four or five inches."

"I'm fine with that."

"Do you want any layers?"

"What do you think?"

Miss Dolly lifted several strands of her hair. "Your hair is thick. Layers will help. Bangs?"

"I had bangs when I was eight years old. Didn't like 'em then. Don't think I'll like them now."

"Come on, then. Let me shampoo your hair first." She motioned to Angie. "Go shop or something. Come back in an hour."

"You sure?"

"I'll be fine, Angie." Mila motioned toward the door. "Go shop."

Miss Dolly took her time with the shampoo and conditioner. Mila closed her eyes and savored the first moments of relaxation since Zane had showed up in town. But once she was seated in the chair with a plastic cape draped over her shoulders—pink, of course—her damp hair combed out, Miss Dolly met her eyes in the mirror.

"Shoulder-length, right?"

"Yes."

"Then here we go."

Mila kept her eyes open as Miss Dolly cut the first strands of her hair. She'd made the decision. She wouldn't be a coward about it.

With a flash of scissors and a quick flick of Miss Dolly's hand, wet strands of Mila's hair dropped to the floor.

Mila exhaled. She couldn't undo her decision.

"You were Mrs. Claus, weren't you?" Miss Dolly focused on her scissors.

"That was me."

"Looked like you had fun at the festival."

"Oh, yeah. Loved handing out candy canes to the kids."

"I meant how you and Ben—I mean Santa—went snow tubing. Great photo in the Sunday paper. I kept my copy."

"That was unplanned." And that was all she was going to say about that. Or the rest of the night.

The transformation was done in under an hour. Angie returned while Miss Dolly blew Mila's hair dry, her salon chair turned away from the mirror.

"Well?" Mila spoke over the whir of the blow-dryer.

"You haven't seen it?"

"Nope."

Angie grinned.

"All done, honey." Miss Dolly turned off the blow-dryer and whirled Mila around.

Her hair hung glossy and straight around her face, no hint of her natural wave, as the ends skimmed her shoulders. "I love it." Mila leaned forward and tucked a bit of hair behind her ear.

"Me too."

"Don't sound so shocked, Angie." Mila raised an eyebrow.

"I'm just glad you're happy. There's no undoing a bad haircut."

"I don't do bad haircuts." Miss Dolly whisked the cape away. "I'd have talked to your friend if this was a mistake."

Mila paid, which included a generous tip, and Miss Dolly gave both women hugs.

Mila walked beside Angie. "Let's get you home so you're not late for work."

"Why don't you change your plane flight? Stay in Chestnut for Christmas?" Angie tossed out the question as if holiday plans had been part of the discussion all along. "Maybe even New Year's?"

"Why?" Mila focused straight ahead.

"Because I know it's going to be hard for you to go home."

"You sound like Zane and I won't work things out." Mila tucked her hat in her purse, still not used to the feel of short hair against her neck.

"I didn't mean that—"

"I thought about things while Miss Dolly cut my hair. I'm going to call Zane again when I get back to the townhouse—"

Angie stopped her from walking farther with a hand on her arm. "Mila, you have to know Ben's in love with you."

"No, he's not." Mila pressed her fingers against her forehead. "We got over all that years ago."

"Maybe you did."

"You're just looking at me and Ben through your happily-ever-after-colored glasses."

"And you refuse to see what's standing right in front of you. I mean *who*."

"I won't marry my best friend—"

"You made that sincere but misguided promise to yourself because of your parents' divorce." Angie stepped in front of her. "But sometimes promises are just attempts to protect our hearts. They're not meant to be kept forever. We grow up and realize the promises we made when we were kids stop us from finding the happiness God has for us."

Angie's words were soft, like the faint whisper of a wind chime on a breeze. Mila tried hard to ignore them, but they settled in her heart and echoed there.

All around her were invitations to celebrate Christmas. Decorated store windows. Banners hung from streetlights. Music danced in the air while the grand tree stood guard over the town center. The season offered such hope—more powerful than a child's wishes for presents under the tree.

Her mother, after all that, still believed marrying your best friend was a good idea. And that love was a risk.

"You're right, Angie. Maybe I made a dumb promise when I was a teenager." The admission eased a bit of tension deep within Mila, something she hadn't even recognized was there. "But it's not like Ben has tried to change things between us—"

Not that Angie needed to know about the what-was-happening moments at the Kendricks' house and at the Christmas Festival. Those were just mixed messages.

"Because he knows about your promise and is trying to honor it, although it's killing him." Angie wasn't backing down. "You could miss out on the best love story—"

"Stop." Mila held up her hand. "This isn't the time to rewrite my romance. I'm your substitute wedding coordinator and maid of honor. And I have work deadlines that are screaming for my attention."

"I'm sorry."

"No apologies needed. Promise or no promise, I'm in love with Zane. Not Ben."

And that was the way it had to be.

CHAPTER 12

Mila opened the front door of Angie's apartment and motioned for Ben to come in.

"You ready to spend our Friday night making the welcome bags for Charles and Angie's out-of-town guests?"

"I'm in." Ben kicked the door closed behind him. "It's freezing out there—wait. You cut your hair."

Mila pulled at the ends of her hair. "No. *Miss Dolly* cut my hair."

"Ah. Chestnut's beloved Miss Dolly. It looks ..."

"Shorter?"

"Beautiful." Ben tucked his hands in his jean pockets.

Ben had told her that she was beautiful before, and his eyes had darkened the same way. Maybe there was more hidden behind that single word than Mila was ready to acknowledge.

"Thanks. I'm still getting used to it. Angie was just glad I didn't dye my hair blue."

"Something smells good."

Mila stepped back as Ben tossed his coat on the couch. "Soup. There's soup on the stove." And surely that was what Ben was referring to. "Do you want to eat first or get to work?"

"You made soup?"

"Ha. Don't be so impressed. It's store-bought, and so are the rolls. I picked everything up when I purchased the items for the gift bags. Chestnut's grocery store may be small, but it's decent." She moved toward the kitchen. "We're here to get things done, right? Charles and Angie are the ones out on a date, remember?"

"Right." Ben nodded. "I'm impressed you talked them into going out this close to the wedding. Do you think they'll relax?"

"All I can do is hope so. I googled 'things to do two weeks before the wedding'—"

"Um, it's Friday, December 12. We're ten days out, remember?"

"The date was on the list for two weeks to go. It took me a week to convince Angie to take a night off."

Ben snorted as he followed her to the kitchen. "Charles was all for it."

"Of course he was. And his oxford shirt was very nice."

"You're welcome." Ben offered a small bow.

Mila ladled potato soup into a bowl. "I had to go over the list of everything we've completed with Angie one more time before she left tonight."

"They've got the marriage license. What more do they need?"

"We visited the church yesterday, so we're all set there as far as flowers and lighting. Charles and Angie still need to finalize their vows." She sprinkled bits of bacon and shredded cheese on top of the creamy soup in both of their bowls and then directed Ben to the two bar stools by the small kitchen counter. "We're eating in here because the table is covered with all the stuff for the welcome bags."

"Makes sense." He settled onto one of the stools.

"And I told her not to make any major changes to their vows this close to the wedding. Her family arrives Wednesday, and then Thursday is our fun day. Spa day for the girls, snowshoeing for the guys."

"Speaking of Wednesday, have you looked at the weather forecast for next week?"

"No. I mean, when I looked at it a couple days ago, it was fine. What? What's wrong?" Mila abandoned her soup, spoon still in hand, and scrambled over the couch for the TV remote on the coffee table.

"Nothing definite yet, but the weatherman said something about a front moving in mid-week that might bring snow—"

"Snow? In the mountains?"

"Here and Denver. You can't be surprised if it snows here. We've had some several days since you've been here." Ben stood beside her as she found The Weather Channel.

"But nothing to worry about. How much snow did they mention?"

"Could be nothing. Could be a lot ..."

His words caused a huge snow-white question mark to hover over Charles and Angie's wedding. Tiny droplets of potato soup dripped from Mila's spoon onto the carpet.

She'd vowed to keep everything under control for Angie, but the one thing she couldn't control was the weather. Mila watched the weather report over and over. It remained the same. A huge *maybe* loomed over the end of the week—and the wedding on the following Monday.

"I'm going to start on a second bowl of soup while you stare at the TV." He tossed the last words over his shoulder as he moved back toward the kitchen. "You've gotta eat, Mila."

"I'm trying to figure this out, Ben." Mila glanced between the TV and the kitchen.

"Figure out what the weather will be in Colorado next week? Good luck with that."

"But snow could affect flights and then people won't be here for the wedding!" Mila refocused on the weather map.

"Angie and Charles are the ones who planned a December wedding." Ben moved around the kitchen. "They live here. They knew weather could be a factor."

"But Denver doesn't usually get that much snow in December."

"Right, but it's always a possibility."

Mila muted the TV. "Angie is going to freak out."

Ben came up behind her and settled his hands on her shoulders and drew her close. "You're the one freaking out right now. Yes, bad weather could happen. Then again, it may all blow over. Literally."

"You're right." Mila still focused on the TV. A part of her wanted to lean all the way against Ben, to let him hold her up, if only for a few moments.

When Ben reached around her, she closed her eyes, but he just took the remote from her and turned off the TV. "Let's eat."

"I'm not hungry."

"Try." He stood behind her for a moment longer, his breath soft against her ear. Then he stepped away. "I'm going to reheat your soup."

Mila remained still as she tried to sort out the conflicting emotions of comfort and longing warring inside her.

Ben took her bowl to the microwave. She'd be lucky to finish any of it. She didn't know what to do about the storm. Or Ben.

The storm—even if it was just a huge lurking *maybe*—unsettled her like that long ago Christmas when her family had been torn apart. And there was nothing she could do to fix what was broken. She opened her eyes, determined to focus on the present problem, not the past.

A few moments later, they were seated on the couch with the TV turned off, their soup warm and sprinkled with fresh cheese and bacon. When her fingers trembled as she held the spoon, Mila released it, letting it clink against the edge of the bowl.

She needed a minute. Just a minute to settle the blizzard-like whirl inside her. But there was no way she could figure this out. "I'm not very hungry. I'll eat some later."

Best friend that he was, Ben knew not to argue with her.

"Okay. I'll finish this, and then we can work on the gift bags. Want to put on a movie? I'll let you pick."

"No. No movie. I'm not in the mood."

Ben rested his hand on hers. "Mila, what's going on? I know you're worried about the weather, but is it more than that? Is it what happened with Zane?"

"No. I mean, yes. Zane and I are texting again. We're not back to normal, but we're communicating, so that's good. And I'm worried about the weather ..." Mila stirred the clumpy soup in her bowl.

"Talk to me, Millie." He squeezed her hand.

Zane. The weather.

She would not talk to Ben about her conversation with Angie.

Could she try to explain the other truth to him without sounding ridiculous? Or pathetic?

Silence stretched between them for a few moments, as the warmth of Ben's touch anchored Mila.

"I don't like Christmas."

There. She'd said it. Her confession seemed to grow bigger, as if it would fill the room like artificial snow from a snowmaking machine.

"You don't like Christmas? At all?"

"Nope." She swallowed against the burn of unshed tears. "I haven't for years. And here I am, organizing a Christmas wedding for Angie and Charles ... deck the church halls ..."

Her attempt at humor cracked.

"But you always celebrate Christmas—"

"I always *fake* it. I haven't put up a tree or lights, but I still drop change in the red buckets. No ignoring the bell ringers." She huffed a short laugh. "Just because I don't like Christmas doesn't mean I want to ruin it for everyone else."

"You've never done that."

"I don't want to bah-humbug my way through December. Nobody else needs to listen to that."

Ben gathered both her hands in his, his touch a welcome relief to the coldness of her confession. He hadn't withdrawn from her, despite what she'd admitted.

"You want to tell me why you don't like Christmas?"

She'd started the conversation. She might as well finish it. Then they'd never have to mention it again.

"You know my parents divorced. Okay, specifics. I was thirteen when my dad walked out. It was the beginning of December—and my dad's announcement that he was leaving was a complete shock. I grew up hearing how my parents were each other's best friend. I loved how close we all were. The laughter. The memories we made together."

Ben knew this part of the story because it had caused their breakup in college. But she'd never told him about the connection between Christmas and her dad.

"We'd always had the best Christmases. We drove around the different neighborhoods to look at all the lights on Christmas Eve. We made a big breakfast on Christmas morning. We went to church service. I would squeeze between them and listen to them sing together. Mom made us stockings. Mine had a little elf, and hers had a Christmas tree, and my dad's had a snowman ... and the tree with all our special ornaments ..."

It had been years since she'd ventured near these memories. With the mention of each one, the ache in her heart sharpened like the broken pieces of one of her mother's delicate Christmas ornaments when it fell to the ground.

"What happened after your parents' marriage broke up?" Ben's question was gentle.

"That first Christmas? I didn't see my dad until after New Year's. I guess my parents decided I'd spend the day with Mom that year. After we opened some presents, Mom spent the rest of the day crying in her bedroom."

"What did you do?"

"I wanted to do something to make Mom happy. She'd bought a fake tree, but we hadn't put it up. I lugged it in from the garage and tried to assemble it myself. That was a complete fail."

Trying to put that tree together—to match the wiry stems into the right holes—mirrored her life for years to come. Out of order. Messy.

Angie's townhouse was as quiet as her home had been all those years ago. Except then, the muffled sounds of her mom's sobs had broken the silence as Mila had wrestled with the branches of the Christmas tree, the fake pine needles scratching her skin.

Christmas seemed so meaningless when her heart was breaking. And here she was, having to do it again all these years later.

"You haven't liked Christmas since you were *thirteen?*"

"Nope. Mom gave up on our family traditions—not that I blame her."

"I can understand why you wouldn't like Christmas."

"What?" Mila searched Ben's eyes.

"I said I understand. Something like that would ruin Christmas for me too."

"You aren't going to tell me how horrible I am?"

"Mila, you've been celebrating Christmas even though it's the most painful time of year for you."

"But I've faked it."

"You've been incredibly unselfish."

"I'm not that good of a person."

"Your actions would say otherwise, Maxwell." Ben pointed to her. "You overlooked your pain and celebrated Christmas for your friends. You always find us the best presents. You even buy Charles ugly sweaters."

That made her laugh. "But I still don't like Christmas."

Ben intertwined their fingers, the touch both comforting and intimate. "Maybe this is the year to change your mind."

"I don't think I'll throw tinsel and lights around my apartment this year."

"I'm not suggesting that. Don't even fake it and put up the wreath on your door. The first Christmas wasn't all that fancy. No tinsel. No lights. No inflatable figures. Although there were angels who had some fanfare for the shepherds."

"Why didn't ..." Mila stopped.

Ben arched an eyebrow. "What?"

"Why didn't God save my family all those years ago?" Her voice trembled, and she could only hope she didn't sound like a grief-stricken thirteen-year-old. "I prayed and prayed for my dad to come home, and he never did. He started a new family. New wife. New kids."

"That was your father's mistake, Mila. God wanted your dad to come back home to you and your mom just as much as you did. And God never walked away from you."

"Sometimes it seemed like He just ignored me when He didn't answer my prayer."

"Your dad made his choices. Wrong choices." Ben rubbed a hand across his jaw. "But what your dad did doesn't change who God is."

"I don't understand."

"I think sometimes we lose God—Emmanuel, God with us—because of all the stuff we pile on Christmas. All our expectations for it to be perfect." Ben shifted closer. "Maybe instead of ignoring Christmas, you simplify it. Focus on the one truth of God as Emmanuel. Just that. See if Christmas means more to you if you let it be about less."

"Simplify Christmas, huh?"

"God heals heartache, Mila. That's the whole point of Christmas—God stepped into our messy world on His journey to bring us back to Him. To give us peace."

With his words, Ben offered her a long-awaited gift.

Mila needed him to understand something. "It's not that I stopped believing in God, Ben. It was just harder and harder to trust Him."

"Because you couldn't trust your dad. It's understandable." He brushed her hair back from her face.

"This is a little scary, Ben."

"I know." His voice was low. "But a lot of good things ... a lot of the best things are scary."

"You're a good friend, Ben Kendrick, you know that?"

His smile seemed hesitant, and then he winked. "Your best friend, right?"

"Absolutely." Mila leaned in and gave him a hug and rested her head on his broad shoulder. Why did being close to Ben feel so right? "Thank you for telling me what I needed to hear. Maybe for the first time in a long time, I'll find a reason to like Christmas again."

"I hope you do, Mila. I hope you do." Ben's strong arms embraced her.

Mila pulled back before any music could start. *None of that.* "Now let's get those welcome bags ready for the wedding guests."

"Can I have another bowl of soup first?"

"A third? Ben, we'll never get anything finished if you eat soup all night long."

"I promise, I'll finish this bowl fast and we'll get right to work."

"While you do that, I'm going to turn the TV back on—"

"No, you are not." Ben swiped the control. "Just wait here. Relax, okay?"

"I'll try." Mila leaned back against the couch and stared at the darkened screen.

"Love is a risk."

Who loved more, though—the person who took the risk, like she had tonight with Ben when she shared her deepest hurt? Or the person who rescued the one at risk, like Ben had done when he'd been her safe place tonight—and then pointed her to even greater safety?

CHAPTER 13

Ben hadn't been back to Ruby's art gallery since the day he'd asked her to be his plus-one for the wedding. He was outside the shop now, a mere nine days until Charles and Angie got married. The Christmas tree still anchored the display, but Ruby had added other items alongside the angel sculpture, including several smaller watercolors on easels and a few pieces of pottery.

Today wasn't about standing outside. He had business inside—with Ruby.

As a customer exited the shop with a purchase, Ben entered to the sound of the electronic chime. Several other people were in the gallery, and Ruby stood at the register at the back, handing a woman a bag labeled Eye of the Beholder.

Ben gave a quick wave when she looked his way, her eyes widening as if surprised to see him.

What? Did she think he might be here to ask her out on another date? Or cancel the one they already had scheduled?

No need to worry about that. Not that Ruby wasn't worth a second date. Or even a third. Mila had talked him into the first one—and she was the reason there wouldn't be a second. But Ruby didn't need to know that. Ben hadn't asked her out on a *dare*. Not exactly.

"Excuse us."

The two words yanked his attention away from Ruby to the Whitmans, who stood right in front of him.

Mr. Whitman motioned past him with his cowboy hat. "If we could just—"

Ben was blocking the door.

"Sorry about that." He stepped forward with a shake of his head and then continued to where Ruby waited by the store counter. "I'm not making it easy for your customers to leave the store."

"I would say thank you, but I don't usually try to make a sale by barricading the door."

"I'll keep that in mind."

"Would you like a water?"

"No, thanks. I stopped by because you emailed you had some gift suggestions for Angie and Charles."

"Oh, right." She moved around the desk. "I thought of two things, based on what Angie said when she's been in. You never gave me a price range, so don't feel obligated to buy anything."

"I appreciate your help."

Ruby stopped in front of a watercolor of an aspen grove hung on a wall near the front of the store. "Angie's commented on this several times. It's by a Colorado artist. I think she said it would look nice in their living room."

"Definitely an option."

"Then I thought about something a little more practical." As Ruby moved away from the painting, the bell over the door sounded as someone entered the shop.

Mila.

"Hi, Ruby ... and Ben?" Mila stopped as the door shut behind her. Midday sunlight streamed through the front window, touching Mila's hair with soft golden highlights. "What are you doing here?"

"I'm looking for a wedding gift for Charles and Angie."

Ruby patted Ben's arm. "You might say I'm Ben's private shopper."

"Oh really?"

"Ruby already recommended a watercolor and was about to show me something else."

"Can I see, or is this a truly private shopping trip?"

"Of course you can come." Ruby scanned the store. "Let me check on my other customers for a moment."

Mila hung back after Ruby walked away, her long multicolored skirt swaying around her legs. "You sure it's okay if I tag along with you and Ruby?"

"Tag along? What do you mean?" Ben motioned around the store. "It's a public place. I'm a customer."

"Doesn't mean you can't get to know Ruby better, Ben. I'm happy to come back later if—"

"Don't start with that." Ben kept his voice low, his eyes trained on Ruby, who still talked with interested customers. "You know better than anyone why I asked her to be my date for the wedding. Today I'm simply asking her to help me find a gift because I know Angie loves this place. Seemed an easy option."

"Dating a nice woman like Ruby could make your life easier too—"

"Stop trying to manage my love life! Here she comes!" Ben stepped up to meet Ruby. "Next suggestion?"

Ruby included Mila in the conversation as she led them over to a display of pottery. "I was telling Ben I thought of something more practical for a second gift idea. Multiple options here. Pottery bowls. Pasta dishes. A mixing bowl set. Even a set of mugs."

"Oh, I love pottery like this." Mila selected one of the handcrafted mugs of blues and browns.

"I've seen you and Angie stop by this display quite often."

"To be honest, it's usually because I drag her over here, although she has mentioned a few pieces she likes." Mila held the mug out to Ben. "Wouldn't you like to drink coffee out of this?"

"Sure."

And now they were talking about what Mila liked as she turned the mug around in her hands.

Nope. Wrong focus.

"The watercolor." Ben's words were abrupt.

"What?" Ruby held a large cream-colored platter.

"I, um, I like the painting of the aspens."

"I didn't tell you how much it is."

"You said Angie loves it. I'm sure Charles will too." He glanced at his watch. "I'm sorry, but I need to get back to work. Can I call you and pay for it over the phone?"

"That's fine." Ruby set the platter back on the display shelf. "I'll wrap it for you too."

"I appreciate that, thanks. I'll see you on the twenty-second."

"Looking forward to it."

"See you later, Mila?" Ben paused between the two women.

"Probably. There's always something wedding-related we need to discuss." Mila and Ruby followed him to the front door. "That's why I'm here—to talk to Ruby about the honey jar reception favors."

Ruby's smile widened. "I have the jars and the labels in my office. The ribbons you wanted too."

"Perfect. I can't wait to see everything."

Ben did not want or need to be part of this conversation between those two women. "I'll let you get to it then." With a nod, Ben escaped.

Mila and Ruby together was a bit more than he wanted to deal with at the moment. Mila, the woman he wanted to fall in love with him and Ruby, the woman Mila kept trying to convince him to date.

Didn't he have a say in the matter?

Lord, have mercy.

CHAPTER 14

As predicted, snow had arrived in Chestnut. This morning the flakes had been intermittent, but more accumulation was expected as the day went on. Tonight, the town would be picturesque, holiday lights glittery against all the white.

Today had been all about relaxation. A pedicure. A manicure. Chips and queso and brisket tacos at Calidad, a delicious preview of Angie's wedding reception in four days.

And now, with lunch finished, they were on their way to massages.

As far as Mila was concerned, today made all the work of being both substitute wedding coordinator and maid of honor worth it.

"How convenient that we can walk everywhere today." Cheryl, Angie's mom, tucked her arm through Fiona's as they strolled through town, the sidewalks salted for the convenience of shoppers.

Fiona, an Angie mini-me with the same auburn hair, did a little double step. "I don't even mind that it's snowing."

"Angie, you've survived your wedding coordinator's pre-term labor, your photographer's broken wrist, and weather travel delays." Mila walked alongside her friend. "Do you now believe your wedding is going to happen?"

"Yes." Angie grinned and tightened the white knit scarf around her neck. "Especially now that our families are finally here. And most of the other out-of-town guests too."

"It was nice of Charles to contact Noah and say he'd pay our lunch bill."

"He's the best. And it's nice to be friends with the owner."

"And that's why you're—" The ring of her phone in her purse cut off her reply.

Ben.

Why was Ben *calling* instead of texting?

"You all go ahead. I need to answer this."

Angie paused. "Everything okay?"

"Yes." Mila waved her on.

Everything was okay. It had to be.

Mila turned her back on the group.

"Is Charles okay?"

"Charles is okay."

Their words crisscrossed each other.

Ben huffed out a laugh. "Knew you'd be worried about Charles. Told you I wouldn't let anything happen to him. Now stay calm."

"What?" Mila's raised voice drew the attention of a couple as they passed by, but Angie and her mom and sister were too far down the sidewalk to hear.

"Calm, Mila. Calm. Where's Angie?"

"She's on the way to the spa with her mom and her sister. Ben, what's going on?"

"There's been a little accident—"

"You *wrecked* your Jeep?"

"The Jeep is fine, but we're headed back to Chestnut so I can see my dad."

Mila's breath formed a huge white cloud as she collapsed against the side of a building. "What happened?"

"I fell on a steep part of the path. Didn't realize it was icy. Stupid of me. I just didn't see it."

"Please tell me you didn't break your leg."

"I didn't break my leg. I think it's just a bad ankle sprain."

"Oh, Ben. How did you make it back to your car?"

"Slowly. Charles wanted me to go to the ER, but we didn't need to do that. Dad or Cole can handle it just fine. If I need an x-ray, they have a portable machine there."

"Maybe you should go to the ER anyway."

"Mila, I'm fine."

"Says the man who doesn't know if he broke his ankle."

"It's not broken." Ben's voice was firm. "How are things there?"

"We just finished lunch."

"Don't say anything else. We're surviving on beef jerky and trail mix. We'll grab something to eat after I get checked out."

"Please text me when you get back in town."

"You'll be busy with your spa day. Text me when you're done."

"Did Charles call Angie?"

"No. He agreed if I talked to you, that was good enough."

"I assume he's driving."

"Yep. Now go get a sushi wrap or whatever kind of massage you like."

Now she had to laugh. "I don't even like regular sushi, much less any rubbed on my body."

"Made you laugh."

"I expect a text when I'm done."

"I expect a text when *you're* done."

They were at a stalemate. Mila pushed away from the wall, the brick rough against her palms. She'd forgotten the gloves Ben had gifted her when he'd picked her up at the airport.

After a few steps, she paused and typed a text to Ben.

AH4UM

...AH4UB

My turn to take care of you. Don't argue.

Don't worry about me. Go have fun.

Please text me. Love you.

...I love you too.

But ninety minutes later, Ben hadn't texted her.

She should have just gotten up from the massage table with a polite "Thanks, but no thanks" because during the entire ninety minutes of her appointment her mind had whirled around like the little wheel of death on a computer screen.

At least now she could check and see where Ben was while Angie enjoyed her facial add-on and her mom and sister visited some of the shops.

"Are you okay if I run an errand? I need to go check on something."

Errand was stretching things a bit, but she did have to check on something. And someone.

"We'll be fine." Fiona gave her a hug. "We'll meet Angie here when she's finished."

"I should be back in time. I'll text Angie."

Mila hiked up the main road through the center of town past the Christmas tree to the Kendricks' medical practice, the location proclaimed by Kendrick Family Practice engraved on a large boulder. Behind it stood the late nineteenth-century house where Ben's father and older brother saw patients. But Ben's Jeep wasn't one of the vehicles parked out front.

Had they left already?

Mila hurried up the wooden steps, across the front porch, and into the front rooms that had been opened into one space to work as the waiting room. Off to one side, Ben's mother stood behind the desk talking to the receptionist.

"Mrs. Kendrick!"

"Mila." Ben's mom smiled. "Let me guess. You're here to check on Ben."

"You would be correct." Mila leaned against the countertop. "Is he still here? I didn't see his Jeep out front."

"Just finishing up. Charles drove the others home and said he'd pick up Ben when he was done. I'll take you to see him."

"Really?"

"Of course." She motioned for Mila to follow her down the hallway lined on both sides with exam rooms.

"His ankle isn't broken, is it?"

"No, just a bad sprain. Cole confirmed it with an ultrasound." She stopped outside a room, rapped on the door, and then eased it open. "You have a visitor, Benjie."

"A visitor—?" Ben rose from the exam table. "Mila! What are you doing here?"

"You didn't text me."

"I told you to text when you were done."

"And I told you to text me when *you* were done."

His mom laughed. "I'll leave you two to figure out who was supposed to text whom. Just remember my son is injured, please."

"Yeah, I'm injured."

"It's your ankle, not your hand, *Benjie*."

"I like it when my mom calls me that." Ben crossed his arms and leaned against the exam table. "You are not my mom."

"I was worried about you." Ben looked fine except for the black walking boot that went up his leg mid-calf.

The urge to hug him had built as she walked through town, and Mila lunged forward and wrapped her arms around him. The only problem was that Ben's arms were still crossed against his chest, which caused an awkward half hug.

With a soft chuckle, Ben untangled his arms and gathered her close so her nose was pressed against the soft flannel of his shirt, her head tucked under his chin. "Whoa. What's that for?"

"I was worried about you, you doofus. What do you think?"

"Mila, I'm fine. I need to wear a boot and stay off it for a couple of days, but I'll be okay for the wedding." His arms tightened around her as she shifted against him, and his voice rumbled in his chest against her ear. "More embarrassed than anything. Who slips snowshoeing? I am a doofus."

"You're not a doofus."

"Make up your mind."

Mila leaned back and tilted her head up. "Next time I tell you to text me, text me."

"Aren't you the bossy one."

"Only when I'm worried about you."

"Thank you for caring."

"I do care about you, Ben."

At her words, the air between them stilled. "Mila ..."

As he whispered her name, it seemed to cue the first chords of "Mistletoe." Neither of them moved even as the *only friends* barrier faded.

If Ben kissed her now, she wouldn't stop him.

His gaze locked on hers, and Mila rose on her tiptoes as Ben shifted so their breath mingled as he whispered her name again. When his warm lips settled against hers, she lost herself in the alluring familiarity. His kiss satisfied the longing that had been building inside her for days—one she'd tried to ignore.

She'd missed this.

A sharp knock on the door pulled them apart just before Cole Kendrick walked in.

"I just double-checked—hey, Mila! I didn't realize you were here." Cole stopped a few steps inside the room. His dark eyes behind his glasses flicked between the two of them. "Did you come to pick Ben up?"

"Um, no. No." Mila shook her head, unable to meet Cole's eyes. "I was in town and Ben hadn't texted an update, so I walked up to see how he was. He seems fine. You're fine, right?"

"Yep. Fine."

"I imagine he is."

Cole's grin reminded Mila that Ben held her—and she held him. Did Cole suspect what he'd interrupted? She shrugged out of Ben's arms. "I meant his ankle. His ankle is fine."

Ben pointed at the walking boot. "Except for a bad sprain."

"I can confirm that." Cole became businesslike. "I came to tell you that the x-ray Dad took to confirm the ultrasound findings also didn't show a fracture. You have a grade two, lateral ankle sprain—"

"Blah, blah, blah. What do I need to do?"

"Wear the boot for a couple of days. Keep your foot up as much as possible to reduce swelling. In a few days— hopefully by the wedding—you can transition to a stirrup splint."

"I'll let you two finish up." Mila backed toward the door.

"Mila, wait—"

"Your mom said Charles is going to pick you up. No need for me to hang around."

Mila fast-walked through the office. Her footsteps pounded across the porch and down the steps dusted with snow, and then crunched on the gravel parking lot. The snow was heavier now and coated the parked cars, trees, and the ground.

She could use a redo on that massage.

No. She wanted to climb in bed, pull the covers up over her head, and sleep until the New Year.

Not that it was an option. She couldn't skip Angie and Charles's wedding.

Maybe she could just sleepwalk down the aisle.

But first she had to text Angie and let her know she'd walk back to her townhouse and meet everyone there.

Mila pounced on Angie the minute she came home an hour later.

"I need to talk to you." She tugged her toward the stairs. "Now."

"Mila—my mom and sister ..."

"It's fine, Angie." Her mom waved them off. "This seems urgent."

"It is. Thanks for understanding."

Mila ushered her friend into the guest bedroom and locked the door behind them.

"Isn't that a bit much? Do you think my mom will barge in on us?"

"Sorry. I'm overreacting." Mila pressed her fingertips against her temples and closed her eyes. "I need you to tell me that I love Zane."

Silence.

Mila opened her eyes. "Angie, tell me that I love Zane."

"Why do I have to tell you that?"

"Because ... because ..." Mila groaned. "Never mind."

Angie squeezed into the small space between Mila and the bedroom door. "You do not drag me upstairs and lock me in this room and then order me to tell you that you love some guy who got mad at you for being a wonderful friend and then say 'Never mind.'"

"It's ridiculous."

"Tell me what is going on, Mila."

Mila closed her eyes again, exhaled, then stared over Angie's shoulder. "Sometimes when I'm near Ben ... when he hugs me, or I hug him ... I think I hear music." She stepped back. "I'm crazy, right?"

"What kind of music?"

"The romantic Christmas kind."

"Interesting." Angie's lips curved in a knowing smile.

"Don't say 'Interesting' like that. It doesn't mean anything." Mila stiffened her shoulders. What would Angie say if Mila told her about that kiss? Not happening. "I love Zane."

"Do you hear romantic Christmas music around him?"

"No, he's much too practical for that—"

"Do you hear yourself?" Angie grabbed both of Mila's shoulders. "Are you really in love with that guy?"

"I can't be in love with Ben!"

"Why not? Because he's your best friend? That's exactly *why* you're in love with him."

"I'm not ... I *won't* fall in love with Ben Kendrick."

"I'm not talking about falling in love with Ben. I'm talking about the fact that you *are* in love with him. That you fell in love with him years ago. A decade ago, to be precise."

It was like someone stepped into the middle of their conversation with a huge red STOP sign. Mila's denial stalled in her throat as the words piled up behind one another like a verbal traffic jam.

Angie might be right.

Angie couldn't be right.

CHAPTER 15

Mila hadn't expected to be sitting at a corner table in Chestnut's Roasting on the Saturday before Angie's wedding.

Not until Zane had called her yesterday morning.

"It's nice to hear your voice." Mila had set her laptop on the bed.

"Nice to hear your voice too." Zane cleared his throat. "I know things are still a little strained between us—"

"You'll be here in two days."

"That's why I'm calling you."

Mila stood, the wood floor cold against the soles of her bare feet. "You're still coming for the wedding?"

"Yes, but I wanted to come out Saturday. Tomorrow. I hoped we could have a little bit of time together."

Mila had chewed her bottom lip. "I'll still be busy then, Zane."

"I understand. But if you think you could spare a couple of hours, I'll book the flight pulled up on my computer." He'd given a short laugh. "I know better than to pull a surprise visit to Chestnut again."

Now, the coffee shop overflowed with people in search of a caffeine fix to help them finish their Christmas shopping. The constant hiss of the commercial espresso machine warred with the overload of voices and pungent aroma of coffee beans. She'd arrived early to meet Zane, only to find all the tables and chairs occupied, and waited ten minutes to claim this tiny spot of privacy when two people left.

Ever punctual, Zane arrived right on time. Their embrace was brief and then they sat across from each other. When Zane stretched his arm across the table, she placed her hand in his.

Mila nodded toward the front. "You want coffee?"

"Maybe when the line dies down."

"You mean *if*. It's remained that long since I've been here."

"Well, I'm here to see you, not for the coffee." He rubbed his thumb across the back of her hand. "It's so good to see you, Mila."

This almost reminded her of their first date, except something was missing. The anticipation. She'd had no reaction to Zane's touch. No warming of her skin.

Maybe she just needed a moment.

How could she think that after what had happened with Ben on Thursday?

"I wanted to apologize for how things have been." Zane tapped the back of her hand with his thumb. "I overreacted about the office party when I was here before."

Mila waited for him to add "and about Ben."

Nothing.

"You've already apologized, Zane."

"Yes, but now I can do it face-to-face."

"I forgive you." She tapped their hands against the table.

"Good. That's important for me to hear." Zane shifted in his seat as he let go of her hand. "There's something else I want to say to you. Ask you, really."

"What ... what do you mean?"

In the next second, Zane pulled something from his inside coat pocket. Set it on the table.

A Tiffany blue box with an elegant white bow.

Her fingers trembled as she tucked her hands beneath the table.

No.

"What did you say?" Zane's words hung between them.

Mila gasped. Had she spoken out loud? "I said ... I said ..."

"No." Zane hadn't moved since the unexpected reveal. "But I haven't asked the question yet."

Mila twisted her fingers together. "Don't ask, Zane."

"Mila, you had to expect ..."

"I know." Her heart pounded in her chest so hard it seemed to be hollowing it out. "But I can't marry you."

Silence met her declaration.

"Zane, say something. Please."

"I was waiting for you to tell me why you can't marry me."

The request? Simple enough. The answer? As overwhelming as the changes in the social media algorithms she tried to stay ahead of for work.

The festive noise that filled the coffee shop couldn't pierce the suffocating *why* that pressed between them.

She needed to be honest.

But how honest?

"Zane, I haven't lied to you. I do love you." Mila ignored the doubt that clouded Zane's eyes. "But I haven't been honest with myself."

"You're talking about Kendrick."

"Ben."

"You're telling me that you're in love with both of us? Equally? Isn't that...cheating?" Zane's hand fisted on top of the table.

"Ben is my best friend—has been my best friend since college." Mila swallowed against the tightness in her throat. "And I've never allowed myself to think about him as anything else."

"But now you are."

"I can't marry you when I'm ... confused."

And she couldn't tell Zane she loved Ben before she told Ben himself.

"I'll wait—"

"No."

Zane closed his eyes for a moment and then looked back at her. "I see."

"I'm sorry—"

"No apologies, Mila." He removed the ring box from the table and tucked it inside his coat. "After all, nothing important happened here today."

Mila stood as Zane rose from his chair.

"You'll understand if I don't come to the wedding?" Zane straightened his shoulders.

"Yes." Tears clouded her eyes.

"I'll miss you."

"I'll miss you too."

He turned away without touching her, but his whispered "I doubt that" wrapped around her heart like a final farewell.

CHAPTER 16

Less than twenty-four hours.

Yes, Mila was counting. In less than twenty-four hours, this rehearsal dinner would be over, all the preparations would be checked off, and Angie and Charles would be married. *At last.* She'd be off the clock as Angie's wedding coordinator and could enjoy being just her maid of honor. Family and friends would be celebrating at the reception, *oohing* and *aahing* over the Mexican food, the gingerbread log cabin groom's cake, the array of dessert choices—not missing the cake cutting at all!—and the tiny bottles of honey they'd take home with them. The local sports photographer had enlisted the aid of his sister, who was in town for the holidays, and who had several years' experience with wedding photography. Thank You, God. All the mishaps would become reasons to laugh.

So far, no one knew about Zane's brief trip to Chestnut and his almost proposal. Right now, life was all about Angie and Charles. She'd simply said he'd ran into a conflict and couldn't make it to the wedding. True enough. Once the newlyweds were on the way to their honeymoon, she'd think about her life. And Ben.

"You're very happy about something." Ben came to stand beside Mila, a plate of meatballs in his hand.

And there he was.

"I am happy." She exhaled a long sigh as she shook her loose waves. "Did I mention you did very well at the rehearsal? I didn't detect much of a limp, not even when we had to do three trial runs up and down that aisle."

Ben raised his pant leg a few inches to reveal his ankle. "The splint helps."

"Will that mess with your suit tomorrow night during your official best man honors?"

"If it does, I won't wear it."

She touched his arm. "Ben, if you need to wear something to protect your ankle—"

"I can always take the splint off for the ceremony and then slip it back on during the reception if it bothers me."

She wagged her finger at him like a schoolteacher. "I'm going to check on you."

"I know."

"By the way, I'm not sure I've thanked you for all your help this past month. From the airport run to the photographer to, well, everything."

"We're a good team, Maxwell." He leaned close. "And don't forget about the sleigh ride."

"Shh!" She looked over her shoulder.

"Don't worry, Charles and Angie are across the room."

"Maybe we should take up wedding planning professionally."

"No thank you." Ben shook his head. "Happy to help Charles and Angie, but everything we dealt with convinced me that I don't ever want to plan another wedding!"

"What about your own wedding?"

"You're the only person I'd want to plan a wedding with." Ben switched the plate back and forth between his hands.

"This is awkward. Where's a table or a trash can when a guy needs one?"

Mila choked back a laugh. This moment of comic relief as he juggled his plate of half-eaten hors d'oeuvres snuffed out Ben's attempt to be serious. She was not ready to talk about weddings. And him. And her. Together.

Yes, she'd told him that she'd wanted to make sure he was okay. That she was worried his ankle might ache, which is why she'd watched him all evening. But she'd focused too much on his broad shoulders beneath his dark leather jacket. His trimmed beard and brown hair and hazel eyes. How often their gazes connected and his smile widened.

She was just concerned for her best friend.

But Ben tempted her to draw a red line through the words *best friend* and embrace the possibility of something more. She wanted to admit she loved him in a forever and always kind of way.

CHAPTER 17

"Twenty minutes to go." As they waited in the designated room in the church, Ben adjusted Charles's white rose boutonniere that tended to list downward. "You ready to be a married man?"

"I'm more concerned about you."

"Me? I've made sure you're in your suit instead of one of your ugly sweaters. Now we wait for the go sign and then I stand beside you and hand off the ring." He patted the inside pocket of his tuxedo. "Got it here, safe and sound. Would you believe I slept with it under my pillow?"

"I'd believe it if you told me that you didn't sleep at all last night."

"My ankle's fine." Ben did a short jog in place to prove it. "I left the splint at home."

"I'm talking about how Zane Halverson didn't show up."

Ben adjusted Charles's droopy boutonniere again. "Not the topic for the day."

"Tell me that you don't think there might be serious trouble between them."

"Mila and I have been too busy with your wedding to discuss her boyfriend." He'd avoided the topic all day and would admit nothing.

"She's still not engaged to him."

He stared at his friend. "You're determined to talk about this."

"He's not here." Charles tugged at his cuffs. "There's been no proposal."

"And your point is?"

It was Charles's turn to adjust Ben's boutonniere. "Time's a-wasting, buddy. Are you going to let her go back to New York and let Zane put a ring on her finger?"

Charles's question hung like a lifeline as the clock ticked down to his friend's wedding. Could Ben grab hold of the rope? This was Charles and Angie's day. But then Charles was the one who had tossed him the line.

It was now or never.

It was now.

"I'll be right back." Ben strode past Charles's dad, who held up his arm and tapped his watch without a word.

"We have plenty of time, sir." Ben opened the wooden door so fast it banged against the wall.

"Go, Ben!" His soon-to-be-married friend cheered him on. "We can always have the quartet play another song or two. Angie won't mind because she'll be watching the whole thing."

After he ran down the hallway and climbed the stairs two at a time—he'd take some pain meds later—Ben stood outside the room where Mila had guarded Angie all day, determined Charles wouldn't see his bride until the processional, accompanied by the strains of "A Thousand Years."

"Here goes nothing ... more like everything." With a perfunctory tap, Ben shoved the door open.

Angie stood in the middle of her designated room in all her bridal finery. Next to her was her mom and younger sister. Mila adjusted the veil that cascaded over Angie's shoulders while the photographer aimed her camera at them.

"Ben! What are you doing here?" Mila stepped around Angie, hands raised, as if she was going to shove him out of the room and all the way back down the stairs to where Charles waited. "Is everything okay?"

"I need to talk to you." Ben stepped forward and lowered her hands.

Click.

"Now?" She tried to tug her hands away, but Ben refused to let go. Not until he'd said what needed to be said.

"Yes. Now. I'm not waiting another minute to tell you how I feel about you, Mila."

Click.

Ben glanced at the photographer. "Are you taking pictures of us?"

"Um, yeah." She lowered the camera with a half shrug. "Just wanted to make sure I didn't miss something important."

"Stop." Mila waved the woman away. "Ben, this isn't the time—"

"I love you, Mila." Ben didn't care if anyone took photos or recorded what he said. "I've never stopped loving you. Yes, you're my best friend, but that fact doesn't make our getting married a horrible idea. We know each other. We understand each other."

"Ben, I—"

"I know you're afraid we'll end up like your parents. But Mila, we decide our future together with God's help—if we're brave enough to risk it. If we dare to love one another."

"Ben—"

He ignored the interruption again. "I get it. You're dating Zane." Ben took as deep a breath as if he were attempting an Olympic ski jump. "But there's been something happening between us since you came to Colorado. Maybe if you're honest with yourself, you might realize you could be falling in love with me."

At last, Ben had silenced Mila. He stepped closer, erasing the space between them, and lowered his voice. "You don't know how much I want to kiss you. But I won't—not until you're sure. And once I do kiss you, one won't be enough." He glanced up at the group of women in the room. "I should go. I don't want to delay the wedding."

Ben exited the room without a glance back. He'd said what he'd needed to say. What he'd wanted to say to Mila for years. It was up to her now and in God's hands.

The click of the door closing seemed to echo in the room after Ben left.

Mila stared at the door until the photographer eased in front of her. "Sorry. I, uh, need to get to the sanctuary."

"Sure. Right." Mila pressed her lips together as she stepped out of the way and then turned to face the other women. All three smiled at her as if they'd just witnessed the perfect ending to their favorite rom-com.

Had anyone else heard the romantic instrumental piano music that seemed to still linger in the background?

Please, someone find the off switch to the soundtrack.

"What was that?" Mila's question was a stage whisper.

Angie stepped toward her, the soft folds of her wedding gown swishing around her feet. "Looks like Ben finally decided to be honest with you. About time."

A knock at the door interrupted Mila's response to Angie's declaration. The church's events coordinator peeked in. "Ready to go? There's a very eager man waiting for you at the front of the sanctuary."

Mila picked up Angie's bouquet of white roses woven with silver and blue ribbons and shoved it into her hands. "Let's get you married."

"Mila—"

"Angie, you've survived so much. Let's do this, okay?"

Angie's mom stepped on one side of Angie as Fiona stepped on the other side. They slipped their arms through hers and moved her toward the door.

The wedding was happening, which meant this was not the time to think about Ben.

She would not fail Angie now. She would put a smile on her face and be the perfect maid of honor. After all, she was good at faking things.

Charles waited for him halfway down the hall. Ben hurried forward. "Are we late?"

"Not yet." Charles slung his arm over his shoulders and moved them toward the sanctuary, as his father and cousin followed behind. "So?"

"So now we get you married."

"That's all you have to say?"

"I told Mila I loved her and wanted to marry her. That our being best friends was a benefit, not a negative, for us to have a future together. End of story. Left everyone a bit shocked."

"I'm sure you did. Angie texted me and said you were there, and I told her that I sent you."

"I'm sure she loved that."

"I'll show you the photos and the stream of emojis she sent me later."

"You'll be busy later."

"We'll all laugh about this later."

"You're optimistic."

"It's my wedding day, man. I believe in happy endings."

"Look at you, Mr. Romantic." His impulsive action was like a bungee drop into the middle of Charles and Angie's wedding ceremony.

As they positioned themselves at the front of the church, Ben tugged at his bowtie. "I should have waited."

"No regrets. You've finally spoken up, told Mila how you feel."

"My timing was off."

Charles stepped in front of him. "I'm the groom and I was fine with you going in there. Angie didn't kick you out. So don't worry about that. Sometimes, loving someone means doing the risky, ridiculous thing."

"Can I quote you?"

"Sure. Now can I go get married?"

"Yes."

Risky. Check.

Ridiculous. Check.

Would he do it again?

Yes. For Mila, he would do it again.

And maybe he'd do it sooner.

Ben shifted from one foot to the other.

Charles leaned back and whispered. "You okay?"

"I'm the one who's supposed to keep an eye on you."

"I didn't just recreate a forty-yard dash in the church with a sprained ankle."

"I'm fine."

"Shouldn't lie in church, buddy."

At that moment, the music changed to signal the start of the ceremony. Ben's eyes never wavered as Mila slow-stepped down the aisle after Fiona.

Mila's eyes were fixed on the pastor as if the man was her true north.

"You with me?" Charles's question was a stage whisper.

"One hundred percent."

That would be the truth from this moment on. He patted the jacket pocket. The ring was still there. Time to be the best man for Charles.

A few moments later, he handed Charles a handkerchief as the man teared up when Angie's father walked her down the aisle.

"You okay?"

"Never better."

The ceremony was a blend of laughter and tears. Laughter, when Charles stepped on the side of Angie's veil and caused her to pull up short as they both walked toward the pastor. Tears, as the two exchanged vows they'd written for one another.

Ben closed his eyes and listened to their promises to live honestly with one another, to trust each other with their hearts and with their futures, to embrace opportunities for fun, to be brave together when they were afraid, and to remember that God promised new mercies for them at the beginning of each day.

As Ben and Mila placed the rings in the pastor's hands, their eyes connected for a moment. How he wanted to be able to make his own promises to Mila. At least she knew that now.

CHAPTER 18

Angie hugged Mila as they stood just inside the doors of the restaurant. The last of the guests crowded the sidewalk as they waited to cheer Charles and Angie before they left for their honeymoon.

"Thank you for everything."

Mila straightened her friend's faux fur cape. "Have a wonderful time in Hawaii."

"Will you send Sybil some photos from the reception? I want her to see the dessert table—"

"I have her email. I'll handle it, I promise. If there are any updates about her and the baby, I'll let you know. For now, we pray the baby stays put as long as possible. The only thing I want you to think about now is your honeymoon."

"You're right."

Cold air rushed into the restaurant as Charles opened the door and took Angie's hand. "Ready to go?"

"I was just thanking Mila—"

Mila gave her a gentle push toward Charles. "Go on your honeymoon with your husband."

"I love the sound of that."

"Which one? Husband or honeymoon?"

"Both." Angie tossed her a quick smile and then disappeared into the group of friends and family, their cheers of

"Congratulations!" and "Have a wonderful time!" drowned out as Charles honked the horn when he drove off.

With the bride and groom on the way to their hotel in Denver before the next morning's flight to Hawaii, the wedding was officially over. Mila was no longer a maid of honor. She kicked off her shoes and bent down to pick them up.

Ah, relief.

Now to find her purse and head back to Angie's for a few hours' sleep before she was due at the airport tomorrow night.

Mila found the nearest chair and sank into it and then dropped her shoes, the sound muffled by the noise of the catering crew clearing away the buffet and the high tables scattered through the restaurant's main room. Some of the guests had come back inside to gather their coats, purses, and tiny jars of honey. In the far corner, Ruby chatted with Cole, who'd come to the wedding solo.

Ah. Maybe some good would come out of tonight after all.

Mila wasn't surprised when Ben approached her, stopping a few feet away. He'd removed his jacket and tie hours ago and rolled up his shirtsleeves.

"Mila, I—"

She stood, their height difference accentuated because Mila was barefoot. "Please, don't say anything, Ben."

The words started the kind of ache in her chest that always eased when she pulled on Ben's gray hoodie. That wouldn't work this time because the hoodie was back in New York ... and because this ache deepened with every breath she took.

Why did the right choice, the only choice, hurt so much?

"Don't you think it's time we talked this out?"

"I-I can't. Not yet."

"Not yet? What does that mean? When are you going to be ready to admit—"

"I love you, Ben."

Ben didn't move. "What did you say?"

"I love you." She closed the space between them and pressed her hand against his chest. "I've known it for a while now—and I've probably loved you for years."

Ben wrapped his arm around her waist. "Then I don't understand why we're not talking ... kissing even ..."

"Can we sit down, please? Talking with you while I'm on my tiptoes is going to hurt after a while."

Ben swept her into his arms and carried her to a chair. He pulled another one close to hers, and sat so close that she might as well have sat in his lap.

Time to talk, while workers cleared the room of the remnants of Charles and Angie's celebration.

"What you don't know is that Zane was here Saturday." She held up her hand before Ben could respond. "He planned to propose. I told him not to because I was confused."

"Confused."

"I wasn't going to tell him that I loved you before I'd told you." When she caressed the side of his face with her fingertips, he captured her hand and pressed a soft kiss into her palm. Warmth spread up her arm, and she could only hope he'd do that again. Soon.

"So here we are, talking this out." He leaned closer with a wicked smile. "About that kissing I mentioned earlier ..."

She pushed against his chest. "There's something I have to do first."

"Before I can kiss you?"

"Yes." Mila pressed her lips together. "I've been thinking about our conversation about my family. My father. God."

"Okay."

"I need to go see my father, Ben."

Ben's eyes widened. "Go see you father? I don't follow."

"I didn't trust God because I didn't trust my father. Even more than that, I haven't forgiven my father for abandoning my mom." She blinked away tears. "For abandoning me."

"When are you going to see him?"

"I need to fly back to New York tomorrow. Make plans." She twisted the hem of her skirt. "I know he's some kind of Realtor and lives in Utah—in Moab—so I'll figure out flights—"

"Moab is five hours from here, maybe a little more." Ben shrugged. "I'll take you."

"What? No." Even though Ben's offer warmed her in a similar way to his kiss, she couldn't accept. "You have to work."

"I'm the owner, remember? It's only open a day and a half before Christmas anyway." He stood, bringing Mila with him. "We get ready, load up my Jeep, and head to Moab."

"We're both exhausted."

"We pack quick. Get some sleep. And head out at six. We'll be in Moab by noon—one o'clock at the latest." Ben bent and picked up her shoes. "I'm here for you, Mila."

Yes, yes, he was. He always had been.

CHAPTER 19

Ben was right. They made it to Moab by noon.

Of course, she'd texted him at four a.m. when she had sat on Angie's couch for half an hour and stared at the front door.

> You awake?

> I've checked my phone every hour because I figured you were. Ready to hit the road?

> You okay with that?

> Yep. Be there in ten minutes.

> Don't honk.

> Don't wait outside. You'll see my lights when I pull up out front.

He drove with her hand in his. Right before she dozed off, he whispered, "I'm praying. God's got you."

Once they pulled up outside the office building where her father worked, she turned to Ben. "Wait here."

"You sure? It'll only take a minute to find a parking space and then I can come with you. I can wait nearby in case you need me."

"I'll text if there's a problem." She leaned over and pressed a brief kiss to his lips. Much too brief.

The building was decked out for Christmas, the fake tree centered in the foyer decorated with gold and red ornaments and white lights. She scanned the directory, found her father's name, and stood in silence as the elevator ascended to the fourth floor.

"Ben is praying. Ben is praying." She repeated the words with each step she took down the hallway.

And she'd prayed all last night when she couldn't sleep.

She opened the door with half a pane of clouded glass. Stepped inside. "Hello?"

A man rose from behind the wooden desk that was free of any clutter. "May I help you?"

Same voice.

"I-I hope so." She moved close enough to see that a series of family photos lined the bookshelves behind him. The other family. "It's me. Mila."

"Mila?"

"Your daughter."

"I know who you are. I'm just surprised that you're here after all these years."

"To be honest, so am I."

He motioned to a low-back seat in front of the desk. "Want to sit down?"

"I'll stand, if that's okay with you." She pressed her hands against the top of the chair.

"Fine."

167

There they stood, a cherrywood desk and nineteen years separating them.

Her father cleared his throat, his face devoid of emotion. "I take it you came because you had a question for me. Or something to say to me."

"Yes. Something to say." Mila didn't blink, as if they were engaged in a stare down contest.

"Go ahead then. I was just going to lunch."

"Right." It wasn't as if this would take all that long. "I want you to know I forgive you."

His eyebrows rose. "Did I apologize for anything?"

His response shoved Mila's words back against her, as if he'd leaned across the desk and pushed her. Mila pressed a fist against her heart and blinked away the tears that blurred her vision. "No. No, but you should have."

With that, she whirled away and walked out of the room.

Where was her phone? Her hands shook and only then did she realize that she'd left her purse in the Jeep with Ben. She was almost to the elevator when footsteps pounded on the tile behind her.

"Mila, stop! Please, stop."

Mila jerked away when her father touched her arm.

Come on, elevator.

"You're right, I owe you an apology."

Ding! The elevator doors slid open. Mila stared inside until they closed. She turned to face her father.

"Thank you for not leaving. Again, I'm sorry for what I said back there in my office." Red stained her father's neck above the white collar of his shirt. "But even more, I owe you an apology for walking out on you years ago."

The longed-for words seemed to echo in the empty hallway.

"I struggle to forgive myself." He stuffed his fists into the pockets of his dark dress pants. "The divorce was my fault. Not your mother's. Not yours. And that second marriage? It ended in divorce too. For the same reason. But you're not here to listen to my life story. You said you forgive me, but first I want to say I'm so sorry I hurt you and your mother the way I did."

"I forgive you."

He bowed his head, as if unable to meet her eyes. "Thank you."

There was no magical joy in the moment. No overflow of love for her father. Just a quiet sense that she'd done the right thing. For them both.

Her father shifted his feet. "Do you want to go get something to eat?"

"Thanks for the invitation, but there's someone waiting for me."

"Would it be okay if we keep in touch?"

"I-I'm not sure."

"I understand." He pulled his wallet from his back pocket and retrieved a business card. "Here's my information, if you change your mind."

Mila traced the edge of the card with her fingertip and then pressed the elevator button again. "Thank you."

"Thank *you*, Mila." Her father stepped back as the doors opened. "Merry Christmas."

"Merry Christmas to you too ..." The word *Dad* hung unsaid between them. Maybe she'd be comfortable with that again. In time.

As the elevator descended, her heartbeat returned to normal. Once the elevator reached the lobby, the doors opened to reveal Ben standing there with her purse.

"I realized you forgot this and didn't have your phone if you needed to text me."

This man.

She took a few steps and threw her arms around his neck. Ben responded by hugging her so tight he lifted her off the floor.

"I thought I'd feel different, happier maybe, but all I feel is tired."

"And you're surprised? You should be exhausted. Think of how hard you've been working all month."

"You've been working hard too. And I slept while you drove here."

"We are not going to argue about this." Ben pressed a kiss on her forehead. "We'll just agree we're both tired."

"Agreed." She rested in the safety of his embrace for a moment and then pulled back so she could see his face. "You said something to me yesterday—"

"What?"

"That you wouldn't kiss me again until I was sure that I loved you." She linked her hands behind his neck. "Ben, I'm absolutely certain I—"

Ben didn't wait for her to finish. The kiss was an intoxicating blend of familiar and something new. Now she could allow herself to savor every moment, knowing she could trust Ben and he could trust her.

Mila pulled away and buried her face against his chest. "I can't believe I walked away from you in college."

"Missed my kisses, huh?"

"I remembered how good you are at this when you kissed me in the exam room."

"*We're* good at this."

"Yes, we are."

"I'm not waiting years for another kiss from you, Mila."
He pulled her into his arms again and swept kisses along her
jawline until he found her lips again and kissed her until a
soft moan escaped her mouth.

Laughter caused them to break apart. A group of women
applauded as they walked up to the elevator. "Looks like
you're going to have a Merry Christmas."

"Thank you and Merry Christmas!" Ben took her hand
and waved until the elevator door closed.

"I can't believe that just happened."

"Want to make a spectacle of ourselves again?"

When Ben reached for her, Mila stepped out of the way
without letting go of his hand. "Much as I love you, Ben
Kendrick, we can't stand around here kissing all day. It's
time to head back to Colorado—and then I need to figure
out my flight to New York."

"I have a better idea." Ben stopped her before they
walked outside the building.

"Do you want to get lunch first?"

"Let's be together this Christmas. I think it's the perfect
time of year to get married."

Mila let go of his hand. "Ben! That's crazy!"

"I'm serious. I'll get down on one knee to prove it." The
next second, Ben did just that.

"Stop." She tugged at his shoulders. "Get up!"

"Marry me, Mila Maxwell. We can elope. Or have our
families join us at the courthouse next week. But if you want
the whole wedding extravaganza—the dress, the reception—I'll wait—"

"All I want is to be with you, Ben." She pressed a kiss to
his lips. "No more waiting. But it would be nice to have our
families with us. And maybe Angie and Charles?"

Ben grinned as he stood up. "Courthouse it is and a little more waiting than I thought. Looks like we have some planning to do to pull this crazy idea off."

"Not a problem. If there's one thing we know how to do well, it's plan a wedding."

EPILOGUE

Thanksgiving Day, One Year Later

No sleeping in today.

"Wake up, Ben." Mila settled on the edge of the Manhattan hotel bed and nudged her husband's shoulder.

Nothing.

"Ben, today's the day. Get moving." Mila tugged the blanket off his shoulders.

"Nope." Ben grabbed at the material as he buried his head under his pillow, the rest of his words muffled.

Mila laughed and tossed the pillow aside. "What was that?"

"I said, what time is it?"

"About four o'clock."

One of Ben's hazel eyes opened. "Four o'clock? Are you crazy? We got everything ready last night so we could sleep in."

"I did let you sleep for an extra half hour." She switched on the light. "Look, I'm already dressed."

"I did not agree to get up at four o'clock—"

Mila pulled up the bottom blanket and tickled the soles of his feet. "Get. Out. Of. That. Bed."

With a roar, Ben lunged for her, the blankets twisted around him. Mila laughed and dodged his attempt to pull her back onto the bed with him.

"None of that, Mr. Kendrick. Today is all about the parade, and I intend for us to have a great spot down on the street to watch the balloons and floats." She tossed his clothes at him. "Now get dressed."

"Yes, Mrs. Kendrick. Whatever you say, Mrs. Kendrick." Ben gave her a mock salute. "Do I have time to brush my teeth?"

"Please do and then I'll give you a kiss."

Ben reached across the bed and pulled her down alongside him. "Only after I brush my teeth?"

She could never resist her husband. "Ben. The parade. We'll be waiting for hours for the parade to start ... plenty of time for people-watching ... and kisses ..."

"I'm going to hold you to that."

"I hope so. It's cold out there today."

"Did you remember your gloves?"

"If I didn't, I know my husband brought a spare pair for me."

"He's a good guy."

"He's the best. The absolute best."

THE END

WITH GRATITUDE

"Not to us, O LORD, not to us,
But to Your name give glory
Because of Your lovingkindness
Because of Your truth."
Psalm 115:1

This is the fun part.

Not to say writing *Together This Christmas* wasn't fun because it was. And then again, it wasn't. Rewrites were a virtual wrestling match and at times I thought the manuscript would win. I'm so grateful to everyone who helped me take this idea all the way to the end. Without them, I would have walked away from this story.

My husband Rob – I know you didn't fully understand what it meant to marry a creative, a writer. But you've embraced it all, from the lingo, to the late nights, to the Instagram reels. (Now those are fun, right?)

My family – I'm a wife, a mom, and a Gigi, which means writing gets interrupted by the real people in my life. My family also understands that sometimes I have to say no because the imaginary characters demand my attention, but they know who I love more. *Them. Each one of them.*

Rachel Hauck – Your friendship encourages and motivates me. You're the best writing partner because you respect my voice and push me past my "can I do this?" fears.

Edie Melson – We anchor each day with a text where we ask each other, "How can I pray for you today?" I'm so thankful for each prayer God's answered and know we can trust Him in the waiting.

MBT Friends (Lisa Jordan, Alena Tauriainen, Melissa Tagg, Tari Faris, Susan May Warren, and Rachel Hauck) – My writing journey started here and I'm so thankful we're still cheering one another on.

Mary Agius – Friend. Walking Partner. Brainstormer. Prayer partner. Neighbor. Doesn't get better than that.

My editors: Barbara Curtis and Lianne March – I trust the two of you to make this story shine.

Jill Kemerer: As the project manager at Story Architect, you made all the details of this book fall in place. Whew!

Cynthia Ruchti – I'm blessed to have an agent who's also an award-winning author and who knows her stuff when it comes to editing a manuscript.

Courtney Walsh – You did it again, my friend! The cover for *Together This Christmas* makes me smile every time I look at it.

I'm reminded again how much prayer undergirds my writing life. Whenever I wondered if I'd finish this novel, I leaned into the prayers of my friends: *Fran, Casey, Jeanne, Kristy, Angie, Dee, Therese, Francie, Sara, Sherilyn, Robin, Renee, Libby, and Jeane.*

Beth K. Vogt believes God's best often waits behind the doors marked "Never." She writes both contemporary romance and women's fiction because she believes there's more to happily-ever-after than the fairy tales tell us. Beth is a Christy Award winner, an ACFW Carol Award winner, and a RITA® finalist. An established magazine writer and former editor of the leadership magazine for MOPS International (now MomCo), Beth blogs for The Write Conversation and enjoys speaking to writers groups and mentoring writers. She lives in Colorado with her husband Rob, who has adjusted to discussing the lives of imaginary people.

Books by Beth K. Vogt:

1. *Together This Christmas* (2025)
2. *Dedicated to the One I Love* (2023)
3. *Unpacking Christmas* (2021)
4. *The Best We've Been* (2020)
5. *Moments We Forget* (2019)
6. *Things I Never Told You* (2018)
7. *Almost Like Being in Love* (2016)
8. *You Can't Hurry Love* (e-novella) (2016)
9. *A November Bride* (2014) and *Autumn Brides* (2015)

10. *Crazy Little Thing Called Love* (2015)
11. *Can't Buy Me Love* (e-novella) (2015)
12. *Somebody Like You* (2014)
13. *You Made Me Love You* (e-novella) (2014)
14. *Catch a Falling Star* (2013)
15. *Wish You Were Here* (2012)

Visit Beth at https://bethvogt.com/

www.ingramcontent.com/pod-product-compliance
Lightning Source LLC
Chambersburg PA
CBHW032142170626
46808CB00006B/2338